The Girl Scout Pioneers
Or
Winning the First B. C.

Lilian Garis

The Girl Scout Pioneers

CHAPTER I

GIRLS AND GIRLS

It was much like a scene in a movie play. The shabby dark room lighted by a single oil lamp if any light could make its way through the badly smoked glass that served as a chimney, the broken chair, and the table piled high with what appeared to be rags, but which might have been intended for wearing apparel, the torn window curtain hanging so disconsolately from the broken cord it had one time proudly swung from, and the indescribable bed!

Like some sentinel watching the calamitous surroundings, a girl stood in the midst of this squalor, her bright golden hair and her pretty fair face, with its azure blue eyes, marking a pathetic contrast to all the sordid, dark detail of the ill-kept room. She took from the side pocket of her plaid skirt a bit of crumpled paper, and placing it directly under the lamp, followed its written lines. Having finished the reading, she carefully folded the worn slip again, and returned it to her pocket. Then she threw back her pretty head, and any frequenter of the screen world would have known instantly that the girl had decided — and further, that her decision required courage, and perhaps defiance.

With determination marking every move, she crossed to the tumbled bed, and stooping, dragged from beneath it a bag, the sort called "telescope," and used rarely now, even by the traveling salesman, who at one time found the sliding trunk so useful. It would "telescope," and being thus adjustable, lent its proportions to any sized burden imposed upon it. Into this the girl tossed a few articles selected from the rummage on the table, a pair of shoes gathered from more debris in a corner, and on top a sweater and skirt, taken from a peg on the door. All together this composed rather a pretentious assortment for the telescope.

But the girl did not jam down the cover in that "movie" way common to runaways, rather she paused, glanced furtively about the gloomy place, and finally taking a candle from a very high shelf, lighted the taper, evidently for some delicate task in the way of gathering up her very personal belongings.

In a remote corner of the room an upturned orange box served as sort of stand. The front was covered and festooned with a curtain, dexterously made of a bright skirt, hung over the sides, and draped from a knot at the top. The knot was drawn from the waist band of the skirt, and tied with the original string into a grotesque rosette. All over the box top were such articles as a girl might deem necessary in making a civilized toilette, except at the knot—where the table cover irradiated its fullness into really graceful folds, falling over the orange box-here, on account of the knob, no article was placed, and the rosette stood defiant over the whole surrounding.

The girl placed the candle on a spot made clear for that small round, tin stand, and then glancing anxiously at the door, stole over to make sure that the bolt was shot, hurried back and proceeded to untie the knot of string responsible for the drapery over the orange box. By the glare of the candle's flame her fingers could be seen stained with oil, and grim, as they expertly worked at the tied-up skirt, and finally succeeded in pulling apart the ragged folds. Quickly she slipped one small hand beneath the calico, and, obtaining her quest, drew back to examine it.

One, two, three green bills. Her savings and her fortune. Lights and shadows crossing the youthful face betrayed the hopes, and fears mingling with, such emotions as the girl lived through in this crowded hour, but no sooner had she slipped the small roll of bills into the flaring neck of her thin blouse, than a shaking at the door caused her to kick the telescope bag under the bed, hastily readjust the cover of the orange box, blow out the capering candle flame, and then open the door. A woman young in face but old in posture scuffled in. She wore a shawl on her head, although the season was warm April, and the plentiful quantities of material swathed in her attire proclaimed her foreign.

"Oh, Dagmar. I am tired," she sighed. "I thought you would come down to fix supper for papa. You do not change your skirt? No?"

"I was going to, so I locked the door," replied the girl Dagmar.

"But I, too, was tired."

"Yes, it is so. Well, the mill is not so bad. It has a new window near my bench, and I breathe better. But, daughter, we must go down. Keep the door locked as you dress. Those new peoples may not tell which is the right room." With a glance at the fair daughter, so unlike herself in coloring, the working mother dragged herself out again, and soon could be heard cliptrapping down the dark stairs that led to the kitchens on the first floor of the mill workers, community lodgings.

Dagmar breathed deeply and clasped her hands tightly as her mother's tired foottread fell to an echo. Love filled the blue eyes and an affectionate smile wreathed the red lips.

"Poor mother!" she sighed aloud. "I hate to —"

Then again came that look of determination, and when Dagmar slipped down the stairs she carried the telescope and her crochetted hand bag. Her velvet tarn sat jauntily on those wonderful yellow curls, and her modern cape flew gracefully out, just showing the least fold of her best chiffon blouse. Dagmar wore strickly American clothes, selected in rather good taste, and they attracted much attention in the streets of Flosston.

Once clear of the long brown building, through which spots of light now struck the night, out of those desperate rows and rows of machine-made windows, Dagmar made her way straight to the corner, then turned straight again to another long narrow street, her very steps corresponding to that painful directness of line and plan, common to towns made by mill-owners for their employees. Even the stars, now pricking their way through the blue, seemed to throw down straight lines of light on Flosston;

nothing varied the mechanical exactness, and monotonous squares and angles of streets, buildings, and high board fences.

One more sharp turn brought the girl within sight of a square, squatty railroad station, and as she sped toward it she caught sight of the figure of another girl, outlined in the shadows. This figure was taller and larger in form than herself, and as Dagmar whistled softly, the girl ahead stopped.

"Oh, you got my note," said the other. "I am so glad. I was afraid you would not come."

"I'm here," replied Dagmar, "bag and baggage, mostly bag," kicking the accommodating and inoffensive telescope. "I hate to carry this thing."

"Oh, that's all right," replied the taller girl, who, under a street lamp, showed a face older than Dagmar's and perhaps a little hard and rough. Just that bold defiant look, so often affected by girls accustomed to fighting their way through the everyday hardships of walled-in surroundings.

"Tessie, I am afraid," confessed the younger girl. "I almost cried when Mama asked me to fix supper."

"Oh, baby! You are too pretty, that's all's the matter with you. But just wait. Hush! There's that crowd of nifty-nice, preachy, snippy scout girls. Duck, or they'll be on our trail," and she dragged her companion around the corner of the high fence, where, in the shadow of its bill-posted height they crouched, until the laughing, happy girls of True Tred Troop, just out from their early evening meeting at Sunset Hall, over the post-office, had passed down into Elm Street.

"I think they saw us," whispered Dagmar, "I heard one girl say some one was hiding by the signboard."

"We should worry," flippantly replied Tessie. "I guess they are too busy thinking about their old wigwagging to notice mill girls."

"Oh, you're mean, Tessie. I think they are real nice. They always say hello to me."

5

"That's because you are pretty," snubbed the older girl, with something like common spite in her voice.

"Here they come back! Guess they lost something."

"We'd better be moving the other way, then. Pshaw! We will sure be late if they keep up their trailing around. Come along. Just be so busy talking to me they won't get a chance to give you their lovely hello. It would be all up with us if they spied us." With a persuasion not entirely welcome to Dagmar, Tessie again dragged her along, this time turning away from the dim lights that showed through the window of Flosston station.

Presently the group of scout girls could be heard exchanging opinions on the possibility of finding something lost. One thought it might have dropped in the deep gutter, another declared she would have heard it fall if it hit the many stones along the sidewalk, and still another expressed the view that it would be impossible to find it until daylight, no matter where it had fallen.

"But I just got it, and wanted to wear it so much," wailed the girl most concerned. "I think it is too mean—"

"Now, we will be sure to find it in daylight," assured the tall girl, evidently the captain. "I will be around here before even the mill hands pass. Don't worry, Margaret. If we don't find it, I shall send to headquarters for another."

"But I shall never love it as I did that one," and tears were in the voice. "Besides, think of all the lovely time we had at the presentation!"

"Now come," softly ordered the tall girl. "No use prowling around here, we can't see anything with matches. I promise you, Margaret, you shall have another badge in time for the rally if we do not find this," and reluctantly the party of searchers turned again in the direction of the village.

Watching their opportunity, the two mill girls came out from the shadows of the high fence they had been trusting to shield them from the view of the scouts. With quickened step they now turned again towards the station.

"Dear me!" exclaimed Tessie. "Haven't we had awful luck for a start? Hope it won't follow us along."

"Well, the more we delay the more I want to go back home," Dagmar replied rather timidly. "Tessie, I am afraid I will not be able to look at things your way. I seem to have different ideas."

"Now, Daggie. Don't go getting scary. I don't care whether you think my way or not. I won't fight about it. Let's hurry," and with renewed protestations of real companionship, the older girl grasped the arm of the younger, as if fearful of losing her hold on the other's confidence.

"Oh, please don't call me Daggie," objected Dagmar, freeing herself from the rather too securely pressed arm grasp. "You know how I hate that. Always makes me feel like a daggar. Call me Marrie. That's American, and I am an American, you know."

"All right, little Liberty. I'll call you Georgianna Washington if you say so, Marrie. That's like putting on airs for Marie. But just as you say," evidently willing to make any concession to have the younger girl accept her own terms.

"Wait! My foot struck something," exclaimed Dagmar, just reaching the spot where burnt matches left the trail of the girl scout searchers. "There, I found the badge."

"Oh, let's look! Is it gold?" They stopped under the street lamp to examine the trinket.

"No, it isn't gold, I think, but isn't it pretty?"

"Kinda," urging Dagmar along. "Say, kid, what is this anyway? A stopover we've Struck? Are we going tonight or some other night?"

"I'll have to give this badge back."

"Why will you? Didn't you find it? Isn't it yours?"

"Of course not. It belongs to the girl who lost it."

"Oh, I see. That's why I should call you Georgianna Washington," with a note of scorn in her voice. "Well, if you want to go back, and get some one to go out ringing the town bell with you, you may find the nice little girl scout who lost her baby badge. As for me—I'm going."

Sheer contempt now sounded unmistakably in the voice of the girl called Tessie. She shook herself free from Dagmar, and darted ahead with determination long delayed, and consequently more forceful.

For a moment the young girl hesitated. She sort of fondled the little scout badge in her hands, and might have been heard to sigh, if a girl of her severely disciplined temperament ever indulged in anything so weakly human as a sigh.

But as the fleeing girl more surely made her tracks to the station, thus leaving the other alone in the night, Dagmar, too, quickened her steps.

"Tessie," she called finally. "Tessie, wait. I can't go back now."

That was all Tessie wanted. She waited, and when again they took up tangled threads of their adventure it was scarcely possible either would allow any further interruptions to delay them.

And Dagmar clutched in her tightly clasped hand the lost scout badge.

CHAPTER II

WOODLAND THRILLS

It was Margaret Slowden who lost the Badge of Merit. The pretty gilt wreath, with its clover leaf center on a dainty white ribbon hanger, had been presented to Margaret on such an auspicious occasion, that the emblem meant much more to the girl scout than its official value of rank indicated.

The True Tred Troop of Flosston had been organized one month when Margaret won the medal. Shortly after the holidays, an event of unusual importance occurred in the mill town, when its small company of service boys returned from "Over There." They were royally welcomed by the entire town folks, together with the many officials of the silk industries, from whose ranks the boys had marched away.

With the lads returned was Margaret's brother Tom. He was handsome and a Marine, and well might Mrs. Slowden and Margaret take pride in the honor their soldier brought them. On the night of the Great Welcome Home, the scout girls, then newly organized, assisted with ushering and attending to the platform needs of the speakers and honored heroes, each of the latter receiving a special small, gold military cross, the gift of the silk mill magnates. This insignia was presented by the most famous authorities of army and navy available, and Tom Slowden was given the special honor of a real military presentation of the D. S. C., he being the only member of Flosston recruits to receive such a notable tribute.

As might have been expected this gave real distinction to the Welcome Home, and Margaret was suffused with pardonable pride. But when she took her place in the check room, to attend to the coats and other belongings of the distinguished visitors—she was forgotten by her troop, and she remained there all during Tom's presentation. She never heard a word of major's wonderful speech, when the people fairly roared for Tom's glory. There she was, downstairs in the dark, lonely cloak room.

"Oh, my dear!" deplored Captain Clark. "I never meant that you should stay down here at this time."

"But it was my task," returned the melancholy Margaret.

"I would not have had you miss your brother's presentation for the world! Such a thing can never come again. Why did you not call some of the girls to relieve you?"

"If Tom did anything like that he could never have received the D. S. C., and I am a Scout and pledged to honor commands," returned Margaret nobly.

For that sacrifice she received from the same platform, one week later, her own badge of merit, and the occasion was a real rally, with officials from headquarters, and all the neighboring troops participating.

Was it strange then that Margaret should lament her loss?

No other badge could actually take the place of that one, and while Captain Clark would immediately advise headquarters of the loss, and order a new one, the brave little scout girl would still feel she had lost that one vested with the special presentation honors.

On the morning following the loss, the girls of True Tred were seen out on the road so early, the station master, old Pete, hurried to his window, and got ready for business, surmising an excursion or at least a local convention imminent.

But no such occurrence was probable, it was only the troop out looking for the badge, and inevitably they did not find it. Signs made by Captain Clark were posted in the station, the post-office, and at prominent corners, but Margaret was disconsolate. She had called her badge the "D. S. C." because of its connection with Tom's insignia, and though the big brother had promised the scout sister all sorts of valuable substitutes, offering her the little hand carved box he had brought for "another girl," and which

Margaret had openly coveted, even this did not seem adequate compensation.

All day at school the girls of True Tred planned and contrived little favors for their unhappy sister, and it was noticeable those of the classes who usually scoffed at the scouts and their activities, could not well conceal their admiration for the spirit of kindliness displayed.

The True Treds had members in the seventh and eighth grammar grades, and the girls' ages ranged from thirteen to fifteen years. Margaret Slowden was fifteen, Cleo Harris fourteen and Grace Philow and Madaline Mower were thirteen. This group was most active in the scout girls' movement, and although the organization was only three months old in Flosston, few there were in the town who had not seen and admired the smart little troopers, in their neat uniforms, always ready to assist in the home or in public at any task consigned to them. It was to be expected they would meet opposition in the way of criticism from such girls as are always indifferent to team play, and the best interests of the largest numbers, but the scouts knew how much they enjoyed their troop, and realized how beneficial was the attractive training they were receiving from its rules and regulations.

Grace and Madaline were still in the tenderfoot class, and wore the little brooch at the neck of their blouses. Margaret and Cleo were already in the first class, and permitted to wear the left sleeve badge, while others showed their rank in the Tenderfoot, the first and third class, three patrols of eight members each making up Flosston troop.

The real work of the scouts is so interesting in character that the writer has no idea of detracting from it, by relating the detail, feeling the charm and significance is best expressed in a real story of the live girls as they live their characteristic scout life. Nevertheless, it may not be amiss to call attention here to the value of such training given almost in play, and without question in such attractive forms as to make character building through its influence an ideal pastime, a valuable investment, and a complete program, for growing girls, who may emerge from the "bundle of habits" as strong members of society, progressive business women, or nicely trained little helpers for the home, or for the more sheltering conditions in whatever path of life they may be selected to tread.

That schools or even homes cannot compete with such training is evident, when one considers that a girl is creative, and should have ample chance to develop her character without force or rigid self defacing, instead of self creating rules; also it must be apparent that guidance is only successful when imposed gently, and with that subtle persuasion, ever aiming to show the result of correct training, and thus affording the principles of freedom for selection, with a knowledge of what that selection will result in.

What sensible girl will deliberately choose to go her own careless way, when she realizes that nothing satisfactory can be expected from such a choice, and that the very freedom coveted makes her a slave to the most cruel limits of prospects or attainments?

But we will not sermonize; even at this distance we may hold out the strong arm of influence, assuring our readers that the highest aims of writers and publishers are for the advancement of the younger girls, whose minds, for the moment, are entrusted to our keeping.

Coming back to our group of Girl Scouts, now holding conclave in the school yard of Flosston grammar grades, we find Grace and Madeline forming themselves into a committee of two, with the avowed intention of getting lip a hiking party for their own special benefit. These younger girls must soon undergo the test necessary for their qualification as second class scouts, and a hike on this lovely spring afternoon would aid them greatly in acquiring the outdoor knowledge necessary.

Margaret was rather inclined to dissent when the jaunt was proposed, she did not feel quite as hiky as usual, and she promptly remembered she had promised her mother some assistance in the little kitchen garden both were developing.

"Oh, come on," pleaded Grace. "If you say you want to go, I am sure Captain Clark will agree. I know where we can get the loveliest watercress."

This lure won Margaret, who had now fully recovered her scout cheer, and was trying bravely to forget the loss of her cherished badge".

"Mother loves watercress," she conceded, "and I would go, if we are sure to be back by five. I have to go call for the mail before dark."

"Oh, goody-good!" sang out Grace. "Now I can surely get my nature work all nicely covered. I'll tell Madaline. She is over there coaxing Cleo," and with a risky flourish of her red tie, a hop, skip and a jump, the Tenderfoot pranced across the big green schoolyard, in a fashion that belied her limitations on the tenderfoot basis.

"Yes, I'll go," Cleo was agreeing, "but I am afraid we can't get Captain Clark. I know she is going out to Kingsley to form a troop. Maybe we can get Lieutenant Lindsley. She is free from Normal at four. They have a lecture after two-thirty almost every day."

"Oh, Lieutenant Lindsley would be lots of fun. She knows everything in hill and dale, and is not afraid of snakes or cows. But do you think we should notify the other girls? It is rather hard to get in touch with them in time," Grace ranted on.

By this time Margaret and Madaline had joined the group, and now all the scouts in seventh and eighth grammar grades were discussing plans for the precipitous hike. There were Mable Blake, also a tenderfoot, Adaline Allen and Mildred Clark, second grades, and the McKay twins, first class scouts. All of these willingly agreed to make the foot trip out to the Falls.

The afternoon school session received scant attention from the prospective hikers, the Tenderfoots especially being absorbed in the prospects of a spring afternoon in the woods.

So interested were Grace and Madaline they exchanged preparatory notes in the five minute rest period, although that time was set aside for real relaxation, and no one was supposed to use eyes or fingers during the short rest.

When school was finally dismissed the girls arranged to pass the homes of most of the group, as many of them lived on the same Oakley Avenue, and thus notify parents of their scout plans for the hike, and when Lieutenant Lindsley was eventually picked up from the practicing department of the Normal School, the ranks were filled, and the hike moved off towards the River Road.

It was a glorious afternoon, in late April. The peach blossoms were just breaking into pink puff balls, and the pear trees were burdened with a crop of spring "snow," fragrant in their whitest of dainty blossoms.

But the still life beauties were not more attractive than the joyous, happy, romping girls, who capered along from the more noisy town streets, into the highways and byways of the long green stretch of country leading to the river brink, and to the woods on its border.

"I'm going to do something really great," declared Grace. "I don't care just what it is, but I want to have a real record, when I am called up to take my degree test. I am not afraid of anything in daylight, so beware! I may do something very desperate and rash this afternoon."

"Spare us," pleaded Madaline. "I have seen some of our courage worked out in the woods before. Remember the time you nearly set fire to the river? Well, don't, please, go try anything like that today."

"No, it must be something for which I should receive a badge of courage, if I were in the first class. I want to blush with fitting modesty when Captain Clark invests me with the next degree, and I shall only blush when reminded of my noble deed this afternoon."

"Since you are not particular about what deed shall be the noble one, won't you just give me a hand, and help me save this heel of mine from a blistering shoe? The shoe was all right in school, but just now it has picked up a snag, somehow, and between the shoe and the snag, my life is not worth living."

"Poor Madie," soothed her chum. "Let us sit right down here and diagnose the case. I'm first rate at diagnosing anything but why my bureau can't stay fixed. It has chronic upsettedness, and all my operations are of no avail. There go the girls down into the hazel nut gully. Let's sit on this lovely mossy couch, and look after the heel. Doesn't moss grow beautifully smooth under the cedars? I wonder how it ever gets so velvety?"

At the twined and natural woven seat, wrought from the uncovered roots of a great hemlock, the girls caressed and patted the velvet moss that formed a veritable carpet—no—it was softer than carpet, a silken velvet throw, over a natural cedar divan. Even the suffering heel was forgotten, in the joy of nature study, in green, with the darker green canopy of cedars, and the music of a running river at the foot of the sloping hill. Here the scent of watercress vied with the hemlock and cedar, for its place as nature's perfume, and only such mingling of wild ferns, trailing arbutus, budding bush, and leafing vine, could produce the aroma of incense that just then permeated the woody glen.

"Don't let the girls get too far away from us," cautioned Madeline. "I wouldn't like to get really lost, even for the joke of having you find me, Gracie."

"But you would do a little thing like that to help me out on my personal bravery stunt?" teased her companion. "I wonder why only the first class girls are permitted to do all those wonderful things and get all the really high honors?"

"Because they have gone through all the necessary trials and examinations," replied Madaline sagely. "You and I can get credit for our deeds, but we must show our full records to get the highest B. C. That's fair. You can't make a major out of a private. He has got to go up by degrees."

"Well, maybe it is fair, but I just love the glory of presentations. I am so sorry for Margaret. I would have dug up the town today to find that Merit Badge she lost last night."

"I like the way she braved it out, though," added Madaline. "She felt badly enough, and it did mean so much to her," finished the sympathetic scout.

"Oh, yes, I suppose so," rather reluctantly agreed the ambitious Grace. "But I shouldn't relish the feeling that some grimy mill girl was wearing the badge in a smoky factory."

"Oh, Grace, shame! That's not scouty. You must not speak so of the mill girls. We hope to take some of them in our troop before long. We would have no right to public support if we did not do something definite for others, and the mill girls have so few chances. So don't, Gracie dear, ever speak like that again."

"I won't if you say so, also if it isn't scouty. I am out to win the goal, and I don't mind what I may have to do to get my scout good conduct ball into the official basket. Now, how's the heel? Did the little pad of soft leaves help to keep the pressure off?"

"Yes, that was a fine idea, and I shall see to it that some day, when original work is called for, you get credit for the nature- aid heel pad. Rather a clumsy title, but when we explain how easy it is to get soft leaves to make pads for suffering feet, I am sure it will be welcome news to many an ambitious hiker."

"Oh, Madie dear," suddenly exclaimed Grace. "Where are the girls gone? They are not in the hazel nut clump, and I can't hear a sound!"

"Oh, my! Suppose they have gone looking for us the other way?"

Both girls in alarm, now scurried through the woods, calling and giving the "Coo-ee" call, but not a sound answered them. Birds were flitting about from limb to branch, and the strange stillness of the woods frightened the little Tenderfoots.

"You go along the bank, and I'll scour the elderberry patch. This wood is so dense in spots, and so clear under the hemlocks, it is easy to lose and hard to find anyone in it," declared Grace. "I'm glad I brought my big rope. I intended to tie every knot in the course, and cut them all out to fetch back finished, and I haven't even unwound the rope."

"If there is anything easier than getting lost in the woods it must be getting caught at whispering in the eighth grade," grumbled Madaline. "I wish my old heel had behaved itself."

"And all the plans for my brave stunt gone to naught," put in the now breathless Grace. "I would never have made up the hike if I had not determined to get a glory mark out of it. Now see where we are! Miles from home, and darkness coming on at each end. Where could those girls have gone to?"

"Sure as shooting they have gone on searching for us. There's the reservoir road, going in the opposite direction, and also Chestnut Hill. To go either of those roads meant getting entirely away from the foolish little scouts who stopped to chatter and chin. Just shows what we can do when we don't know we shouldn't."

For some moments they brushed their way through the thicket, beating down briars with their stout sticks, then coming to a broad clearance they found themselves in a great grove of pines, clean as a floor, except for the layer of savory pine needles, and almost dark as night from the density of the pine canopies.

"My, how lovely!" exclaimed Grace.

"Yes, if we could only enjoy it," demurred Madaline.

"Grace! What's that? Over under that thick tree!"

"A man! Let's run!"

"And there is a big bag beside him," whispered Grace. "See the things sticking out of it!"

"No, I don't want to see anything. Run, I tell you!"

"Wait! Maybe I could make this my bravery act. Suppose I tie him with my strong rope?"

"Grace Philow! Are you crazy?" and the more frightened girl attempted to drag the other away. "Please—don't speak loud. If he wakes I shall die."

"No, don't you dare! Just keep still. I am going to see if I can tie up one town tramp. There are plenty loose, and this is my golden opportunity!"

CHAPTER III

A NOBLE DEED UNDONE

"Now Grace! If you attempt to go near that dreadful man I shall scream and wake him up," threatened Madaline, in real alarm.

"No, you won't either. You would be afraid to. Hush, keep still. I want to see if I can lasso his old bag. Wouldn't it be fine if I could rescue Mrs. Johnston's washing? You know it was stolen off her line two nights ago." With this the daring girl stole up more closely to the sleeping figure.

The quiet lull of the flowing river, as it fell over a little cascade, was acting as a potential lullaby to the wayfarer at the foot of the tree. His figure was grotesque, but at the distance the girls were viewing him from it was not possible to discern more than a figure—it might be that of almost any sort of a man, for all they could tell.

Grace untied her nice clean coil of rope, while Madaline besought her in every kind of cabalistic sign she could summon to her aid, to desist in her reckless intention of tieing the man to the tree. But the temptation was evidently too much for the frolicsome Grace, for as Madaline cast a wild eye over her shoulder in her flight from the spot, she could just see Grace, tip-toeing up to that figure.

A few seconds later came a stifled cry!

"Wait, oh, Madie, wait!" called Grace, and, stopping in the briar path, Madaline glimpsed the imperturbable Grace, making her way through the thicket and dragging something heavy behind her!

"Mercy me!" exclaimed Madaline. "What can she be tugging along!"

"Wait, help me!" now called Grace in a bolder voice.

"No, I will not! Grace Philow, are you crazy?" gasped Madaline.

"Crazy, not at all," sang out Grace in a laughing voice. "I've got it!"

"Got what?" Madaline cried anxiously.

"Mrs. Johnston's wash!"

"Oh, Grace, you will get us both arrested."

"For recovering stolen property! You have a fine sense of scout laws," Grace retorted. "If you don't help me get out of the briars I shall report you to the captain—if we ever find her," and another laugh grated on the frightened ears of Madaline.

"I can't help you, Grace," Madaline replied in a more conciliatory tone. "The briars are so thick here, they almost tore off my shoe— it is not laced tight, you know."

"Well, they are tearing up Mrs. Johnston's wash," admitted Grace, still tagging at the trailing bag, that could not be seen in the thicket and brambles she dragged it over.

"Oh, Grace! There he comes!" screamed Madaline, as a moving figure could be outlined in the shadows of the low brush, and tall swamp berry trees, that just towered high enough to hide the form that bent and broke the impeding young birches. It was the swish and motion of the brush that indicated his advance and location.

"Mercy!" yelled Grace, alarmed now in spite of her boasted courage. "Let's run. But I won't drop this wash. I don't care if he follows me into the post-office for it," and at that, she gave the rope one more terrific jerk, the force of which brought the trailing obstacle out into the path where it had a clear track to follow the girl, who held madly to the other end of the rope.

No words were wasted as the girls scampered and scurried through that wood. Grace held firmly to the rope, and could feel that it still dragged her quarry, while Madaline never turned her head to see whether or not the pursuing man was at their heels. That they had not been struck down was enough, to be thankful for, thought Madaline.

And in all of this, no trace of the other members of the hiking party was discovered. More than once the girls heard something they decided ought to be their "Coo-ee" call, but each time it turned out to be nothing more friendly than the astonished birds, either laughing at the scouts, or rooting for their successful escape from the pursuer.

Beaching the big rock that covered the path, and always had to be climbed over "by hand," the girls scrambled up, then down, and when Grace gave a necessarily vigorous tug at her rope it sprang up to her face in a real caress! In fact it actually coiled around her like a friendly thing.

Mrs. Johnston's wash was gone!

"Oh, he grabbed it!" wailed Grace. "He got hold of my rope when we had to stop to make the rock and now—he has got it again!"

"Don't you dare stop one minute!" panted Madaline. "You have almost murdered us as it is," she proclaimed in her excitement, which always banished her ordinarily sparse supply of reasonable language.

"Nice way you help a sister," mocked Grace. "I thought you were going to help me win honors," and she gathered up her delinquent rope with a much disturbed expression on her pretty face.

"I think I have helped you save your life, if you only knew it,"

Madaline managed to articulate. "The idea—"

"All the same I did tie him up," admitted Grace, bolder now that she could see the end of the woods. "I don't see how he got loose. I used the running bow-line, and a couple of clove hitches. Our old knots came in useful, but they didn't hold evidently. Hark! Wasn't that a whistle! Sounded like Margaret's trill."

"Yes, and it's away over on the Avenue. Whatever will Captain

Clark say?"

"Now, Madie, you just promise you will say nothing about my man and Mrs. Johnston's wash. I tried to do something noble and it didn't pan out, so if you are a good little pal, and a first rate sport, you will keep mam as a clam, won't you, please, Madie?"

21

"Well, since it did not end in a tragedy I suppose I may keep quiet without breaking honor, but you know, Gracie, I am six months older than you, and I would be held accountable at a trial."

"Don't you fret," and Grace was now shaking her curly head and throwing her blazing cheeks up to the clearance light, with, renewed defiance. "I certainly had a lovely time while it lasted."

"There are the girls!" exclaimed Madaline joyously. "It would have been dreadful if they were obliged to go all the way into Flosston without us. They would have come back with the mill bell man looking for us."

"Whoo-hoo!! Coo-ee, Coo-ee!!" trilled Grace, and back came the welcome answer.

"Coo-ee! Coo-ee! Whoo-hoo!"

Realizing the lost was found, Lieutenant Lindsley stood on top of the little hill, just over the turn of the macadam road, that outlined Oakley Avenue, the one street of distinction that ran through the country and gave tone to little Flosston on its way. She was an attractive figure standing there in her plain serge suit, and soft tam-o'-shanter on her finely poised head, and even at a distance one would be correct in describing Romaine Lindsley as an attractive, fine-looking young girl.

Around her were the other members of the hiking party, all of whom had come to an abrupt halt, at the call of Grace and Madaline from the woodlands.

"Don't run to meet them," cautioned the lieutenant, "that might mean another mixup," and she gave a double quick trill to notify the delinquents they were expected to report promptly. "After all there appears to be no harm done, other than the loss of an afternoon's sport."

"But I did not get my watercress," wailed Winnie, the blonde of the McKay twins.

"And I lost a perfectly good side comb mother just received from Philadelphia," complained Cleo. "I wanted this kind and could not get them around here. Now one is lost and the other useless."

"But we must not complain, Cleo," admonished the lieutenant pleasantly. "It isn't good scouting, you know."

By this time the runaways, or lost sheep, had caught up with the awaiting contingent. That they would be deluged with questions, and all but stampeded for answers, was to be expected.

"It was an accident," Grace managed to inject finally. "Madie's foot went blistered—and I hunted around for some—some medicated leaves," this was said in an apologetic tone, "and when the heel was all fixed we were thoroughly lost."

Madaline sighed and smiled alternately, and agreed without venturing to say so.

"Well, we are glad you met with no mishap," declared the lieutenant, to whom girls lost in the woods was not a new adventure. "We were going back for you just now. The trouble was we took the left road to look for you, when, of course, you were hugging due right. Didn't you see our trail?"

"Yes, after we struck it," responded spokes-man Grace. "We were so deep in the cedar grove we had no chance to strike trails. Oh, girls, you should see the wonderful picnic grounds we discovered!" she enthused, with the very evident intention of getting Madaline's mind off the man and the bag of wash. "It is a perfect little park, all carpeted with pine needles, and canopied with the loveliest trees—"

"All right, Grace," cut in the lieutenant. "But come along. We must be making tracks. No time just now for a panoramic view. We will certainly have to take this hike all over again to compensate the girls for their disappointment. However, no doubt we have learned something."

"You bet," Grace whispered to Madaline, as she fell into step for the homeward march. "I learned that the bow-line will slip."

"Hush," begged Madaline. "I am not sure yet but that—you know— may be after us."

"Wish it—you know, was," defied the other.

"What ever were you two up to?" asked Margaret, falling back to take step with the refugees. "I am sure you were never fixing a single foot all that time."

"We each had feet, you know," Grace quickly made answer. "And really there are the most interesting things in that wood. I am going back first chance—"

"You do!" threatened Madaline, with a glance Grace rightfully interpreted. "I will never, as long as I live, go into the Cedar grove again. It's too scary for words."

"I loved it," drawled Grace. "I am going again. See if I don't.

Want to come, Maggie?"

"Maybe, but just now I want an alibi for mother's promised watercress. Grace, you are a great scout! You lure us all out here, with the most tempting offer of prize watercress, and here we go home with a bunch of last year's cattails. What shall we say to all our loved mothers, who allowed us to cut house work for this wonderful afternoon?" asked Margaret.

"Say that I, Grace Gollivar Philow, will go back first chance I get, and fetch watercress for the whole community. Only next time I go, I am going to fetch a gun—"

Margaret laughed, but Madaline shivered. Scout girls were supposed to know how to use a gun, but fortunately Grace was still in the Tenderfoot class. Perhaps before she could possibly get permission to try gunning, she would have outgrown her tendency to capture tramps with ostensibly stolen washes. Madaline sincerely hoped so.

When almost in town Grace gained an opportunity to whisper to Madaline:

"Now remember, Madie. Never a word. I am not sure my man got away, you know. He may be tied up there yet. And also, I may get someone to go with me and reclaim Mrs. Johnston's wash. I know about where it broke loose."

CHAPTER IV

PATHS DIVIDING

But the happenings in the woods were quickly forgotten, at least so far as the scout girls were concerned, by the unexpected development in the case of the two girls, Dagmar and Tessie, who had stolen out of Flosston.

In that section of the town where the girls lived, the Americanized foreigners had little in common with such families as those of the girls of True Tred Troop. In fact, few happenings in the mill community ever reached the ears of the so-called "swells," that inappropriate term being applied to those whose fathers held some executive position in the great silk industries of Flosston.

Thus it was easy to understand why the scouts had heard nothing next day of the mysterious disappearance of Dagmar and Tessie.

A contrary situation existed in Millville, however. Here the families of both girls were causing a search to be made in that peculiar fashion of confusion and excitement, usually ending in making the condition more complicated, and giving rise to absolutely no clues worthy of attention.

Mrs. Brodix, Dagmar's mother, good, kind mother that she was, spent her time wringing her hands and rolling her big black eyes, otherwise in extolling the hitherto undiscovered virtues of the lost daughter.

In her distress she forsook the English tongue, and lapsed into a conglomeration of Polish and Yiddish made intelligible only through the plentiful interpretation of dramatic gesticulation.

"Oh, my beautiful Dagmar!" she wailed. "It is that vile street runner Theresa, who has carried her away!" was the burden of her lamentations.

"The smartest girl in all Millville was my Tessie," insisted Mrs. Wartliz. "It was that baby-faced kitten, Dagmar Brodix, who coaxed her off. She would earn as much money as me" (good enough English for Mrs. Wartliz), "and she had money in the bank, too."

It was probably this last fact that really led the girls to seek what they considered was a broader field for their talent. If Tessie's money in the bank had been a joint account with her mother's name, she would not have been able to draw out the funds for her escapade, but what did Mrs. Wartliz know about such supervision for a daughter, who was absorbing America at one end— the attractions—and ignoring America at the other— honorable conduct?

What actually happened was this. When Dagmar ran after Tessie, who was threatening to leave her to her own resources, that dark night when both had planned to shake the dust of Millville from their well worn shoes, the older girl finally agreed to take Dagmar along if "she would quit her babying, and act decent."

"Now the train is gone," scolded Tessie, "and we have to take that horrid old jitney out to the junction. Like as not we will meet some one who will squeal on us."

"Tessie," pleaded Dagmar, afraid to speak, and fearful of the consequences if she did not make her appeal. "Why can't we go to Franklin? There is a fine mill there and it is nearer home—"

"Say kid" exclaimed the rougher girl, "if you want to go home you have a swell chance right now, but if you want to come with me quit simping and come," and she picked up her own bag in bad temper, gave her brilliant scarf a twist and started off for the jitney, leaving Dagmar to take the unattractive choice she had just mentioned.

Dagmar was too frightened to notice the grimy mill hands who were crowded into the old bus, making their way to another settlement in search of an evening's recreation, but Tessie slunk deep down in her corner, burying her face in her scarf and hiding her eyes with her tam. She knew better than to run the risk of having her cross father discover her in flight. After she had succeeded in getting away Lonzo Wartliz would not spend time to go after her, but while she was "on the wing," so to speak, he would have no trouble in bringing her back. A day's time from the mill would be too costly a sacrifice to make, while a police call to "fetch back my girl" would cost him nothing. Also there was the thought that Tessie might fix it at home by sending a letter filled with glowing promises of good money — but she would require at least one day to mail her promise to Flosston.

So Dagmar sat with a melancholy expression on her face while

Tessie hid her silent chuckles in her wearing apparel.

"Here we are," whispered the latter, as the jitney jolted to a standstill. "Don't forget your Saratoga."

Dagmar dragged the hated "telescope" after her, as she dropped down from the rickety high steps of the old motor wagon. It was very dark now, and she was more frightened than she had any idea of betraying to her companion. "Come on, kid," called the other. "We have got to hunt up something. We may not get out of this great white way to-night."

"Oh, Tessie! How could we stay in a place like this?"

"Just like the other folks. Do you think they are goin' to spread out a wedding canopy for you? Oh, be a sport, Daggie. Tomorrow is yet to come."

The training this young girl had received in the local movies was now developing in a rather dangerous way. She was breathing heavily in her new found adventure, she was out alone, or as good as alone, in a strange place on a dark night, and perhaps she would be kidnapped? In spite of the danger Tessie fairly thrilled with the possibility, and it was with a very pronounced degree of scorn that she regarded her weaker companion.

Not that the "movies" were exerting any better influence on Dagmar. In fact it had been their uncertain propaganda that first created in her breast the feeling of unrest, that first told her Millville was mean, shabby, and an unfit place for an ambitious girl to try to exist in. Her very love for her mother and father, to say nothing of her affection for the other members of her family, seemed a spur to her ambition "to get away and be somebody."

But the getting away was by no means the pleasant dream she had pictured it. Here they were, two young, inexperienced girls in a strange town, without the slightest knowledge of how they might find a safe place in which to stay for a single night, and even they, with their minds open for adventure, realized how promptly trouble comes to those who openly seek it.

"Let's go down this street and see what it runs into," suggested

Tessie. "Hope it doesn't flop off into a ditch."

"I think we ought to ask someone," put in Dagmar.

"Ask them what?" rudely demanded Tessie.

"Where we can go for the night? Are you sure we can't get a train?

We could sleep in the cars."

"Oh, say, you want a Pullman, you do, the kind we see go by the factory with the coons all dolled up in dish towels," she sneered, now seemingly set upon making things as unpleasant as possible for poor, little, frightened Dagmar. But the latter was not altogether a coward, and the blustering tone of Tessie was not too deep to penetrate. Dagmar pulled herself together and dropped the "telescope."

"You may do as you please, Miss Wartliz," she exclaimed. "But I am not going to tramp these streets all night. I don't want to end up in a nice little rat-ridden police cell. We don't have rats over our way."

"And I suppose we do. Well, Miss Smarty, what do you propose to do? Maybe you wouldn't mind letting your friend in on the game!"

"You know, Tessie, I don't mind slang, and I am not a goody-good, but I am nervous, and I think we would get along better if we both dropped that street stuff. It gets on my nerves."

"Oh, my sakes alive! Gettin' nerves!" and she dropped her voice into the deepest tones of contempt. "I might-a known it. You would be apt to have them with that face. Well, kid, what do you want to do? I don't see no hospital for nerves out this way."

"Tessie! See that man!"

"Sure I do. He's a cop, too. Stop your whimpering and trot along. We're goin' to grandma's," and Tessie grabbed the arm of the trembling Dagmar as she started off with a determined step, indicating a particular objective being sought for.

But the officer of the law could distinguish runaway girls without a full confession from their painted lips. And he promptly started after them.

"He's followin' us," whispered Dagmar.

"As if I thought he was playin' hop-scotch," scoffed the tantalizing one. "Keep movin', we will give his legs a treat, even if he intends to beat us out."

And they did walk very briskly indeed—all the more reason why the officer should follow them!

"Makes me think of tryin' to get away from a strange dog," Tessie had the temerity to interject. "The faster we ran the surer he is to keep snappin'."

"He is sure to catch us," Dagmar said. "Why don't you stop and ask him where we can go?"

"You poor simp. Want him to tell you?" and she almost laughed outright.

"Wait—a minute—wait—a minute!" came the summons. "What's your big hurry?"

They both stopped. Each knew enough for that. The man of the law, shaking that treacherous stick on its red cord, was now beside them. He pushed his cap back to make sure nothing interfered with his gaze. This he fixed scrutinizingly on the two girls. Dagmar flinched, but Tessie smiled in a foolish attempt to gain his good will.

"Where are you two trottin' off to all alone?" he asked finally.

"We're goin' to grandma's," said Tessie, so ridiculously that she almost burst out laughing. She had no idea the answer would sound so silly.

"Oh! you be," he returned, his voice thick with irony. "Is the old lady expectin' you?"

"Well, we didn't say we would be there tonight," Tessie had the audacity to reply.

"No, I thought not," and he twirled that formidable stick almost into Dagmar's scared face. "Well, shall we send her word?"

"Oh, we can find our way," put in Tessie again, attempting to start off.

"Maybe so. But here in Franklin we have a curfew law, and we don't allow little girls out alone so late."

"No?" sneered Tessie. "Lovely town. We expect to take the rest cure here."

"Now, my young lady," in severe tones, "I'll show you where we give that self same cure. Come — along — with — me!"

Quick as a wink Tessie grabbed her bag, and started to run. The officer was so surprised he required a moment to realize she was running away. When he did he sounded his whistle.

And there stood Dagmar, alone, and as the "movies" say,

"Forsaken!"

"Oh, Tessie," she called weakly. "Come back. You have my pocketbook!"

But the fleeing girl did not stop to listen to Dagmar's cry or to the shrill whistle the officer again sent out into the night. She was making tracks so successfully, the minion of the law knew very well his whistle would never summon help — the only other officer in town being "out of town" to his personal knowledge. So Tessie went, and with her Dagmar's pocketbook and the Girl Scout Badge!

CHAPTER V

A FRIENDLY ENEMY

"Now, don't you worry, little girl. You are not like that one running away. I can see that by your manner," said the officer kindly, as Dagmar pressed her handkerchief to her wet eyes. "I don't have to take you to the calaboose, unless I set fit, and I don't."

He touched her arm kindly. Jim Cosgrove hated to see anyone cry, and his kind heart never seemed to interfere with the fulfillment of his duty. When he was kind he had reason to be, and never yet had the higher officials questioned his wisdom.

"Oh, thank you," said Dagmar, when she could find the words. "We haven't done anything wrong."

"Well, it isn't exactly right for young girls to run away from home, and I don't have to wait for all the particulars to decide that is what you are both aiming to do. However, let us go along. My wife doesn't mind takin' a girl in now and then, to save her name from the records."

Dagmar breathed easier. She might even find a place to sleep! Why hadn't Tessie waited?

In spite of the rather unpleasant situation, there was comfort in the thought she would not have to go to some dreadful hotel, or boarding house, and perhaps undergo all the hardships dealt out to runaways in the "pictures." So Dagmar walked along with the officer, unmindful of the sharp looks of the few passersby who happened to be out in that section of the rather quiet town.

"Of course you will go straight back home in the morning?" asked and answered the officer.

"Oh, I did so want to try something else," almost pleaded the girl. "You see, mister, it is awful in the mill end of Flosston."

"Not very good, I'll admit," replied he, "but it will be my duty to send you back."

They walked along in silence after that brief conversation. Dagmar was thinking how difficult it would be to go back home on the morrow, and in the company of an officer! As if the man divined her thoughts, he said presently:

"We will see how we make out when we get to my house. My old woman is as good a help to me as the other man on the post, and better. She helps me a lot with the girls, and I often say she should have had a uniform. Maybe we can fix it so she will take you back home."

"Oh, that would be better," replied Dagmar. "I would hate to go with a man."

"Course you would and I don't blame you. But I must hurry and put you up with Mary. If I don't find your pal I will have to give the word to the next town. Can't have a girl like that running around loose all night."

"I wish she had stayed. Tessie is—not really wild, but she has so much freedom at home. All her folks seem to care for about her is her money."

"Lots of folks are foolish as that, then they have to spend a good lot to make up for getting a little. And the funny part of it is, the girls, who seem so wise, are the easiest fooled. Now, she acted like a real grown-up, but I'll bet my badge she would go along with the first person who offered her a hot pancake for breakfast. They have so much nerve it dries up all their common sense."

"I do wish she had not run away. She is always making fun of me and calling me a baby. But I think, as you say, mister, it is better not to have too much nerve."

"You're right, girl. But here we are. Don't you be the least bit afraid of my wife. She is big and blustery, but has a heart of gold."

The rugged outside of this man evidently hid a heart of his own not far from pure gold, and Dagmar could not help thinking he was the nicest policeman she had ever heard of, and that she had encountered him seemed nothing short of wonderfully good luck.

Turning in at the gate, which even in the night could be seen to form a little arch in vines and bushes, Officer Cosgrove tapped lightly on the door, which was opened before the echo of his last tap had died away.

"Here we are, Mary," he announced to the woman standing in the portal. "I just brought you a little girl—who—is lost. Take care of her while I go after the—other. She didn't take so kindly to Jim as this one did," and with a friendly little push, he ushered Dagmar into the narrow hall, and turned out into the roadway, from whence his light footfall could immediately be heard hurrying over the cinder-covered path.

"Come in, girl," ordered Mrs. Cosgrove. "What happened to you?"

Dagmar was bewildered. What had happened to her? What should she answer!

"I am—away—from home," she managed to reply. "The officer said I could go back tomorrow."

The inadequacy of her reply sounded foolish even to Dagmar, but she was constrained to feel her way. She could never blurt out the fact that she had actually run away from home!

"Oh, I see," said Mrs. Cosgrove with a tone of uncertainty. "Run away, eh?"

"Yes'm," said Dagmar defencelessly.

"Too bad. Didn't your folks treat you right?"

"Oh, yes," hurried Dagmar to correct any such impression as that question conveyed. "But I wanted to help them—all, and I thought I—could!"

Tears were running over now, and Dagmar's courage was at lowest ebb. The motherly woman took the ever-present "telescope," and setting it down in a corner of the pleasant room, directed Dagmar to a chair near the little stove, in which a small light glowed, quite suitably opposed to the chill of early spring.

"Just sit down and I'll get you a bite. Of course you are hungry."

"Not very," gulped the girl, who had not tasted food since she snapped the cover on her lunch box that eventful noon day, when the girl, having agreed with Tessie to leave Milltown, had eaten the dark bread and bologna, for what she supposed would be the last time. So Dagmar was hungry, although her emotion for the time was choking her, and hiding the pangs of actual hunger.

"All the same tea tastes good when we use up nerves," insisted the woman, leaving the room, and presently clicking dishes and utensils in the kitchen. Left alone for a moment Dagmar recovered her composure and glanced about the room. It seemed almost fragrant in its clean freshness. She had never occupied such a room, with that peculiar, bracing atmosphere. The small mantel with its prim vases looked a veritable home shrine, and the center table with the sprigs of budding lilacs, seemed to the forlorn girl something to reverence. The rag rugs under her feet were so spotless, the curtains so white — it suddenly occurred to the girl these things could not exist in the smoke and grim of a mill town. It was the mill — always the mill found to blame for her misery.

"Come on, girl — what is your name?" came a voice from the kitchen.

Dagmar responded and took her place at the table with its white oilcloth cover, and a snowy napkin neatly smoothed under the one plate set for her.

"Molly has gone to Flosston to a Girl Scout meeting," announced Mrs. Cosgrove, helping Dagmar to a dish of home-made pork and beans. "She loves the Scout affairs, and wouldn't miss a rally, even if she has to come home a little late. Martin, that's my boy, will meet her at the jitney."

"Gone to Flosston?" repeated Dagmar. "That's where I came from — that is the corner we call Milltown, it is out where the factories are."

"Oh, I know the town well. Not too nice in spots. But start right in. Drink your tea and eat up your bread and jelly. I'll finish what I was at, and be back by the time you have cleaned your plate."

Dagmar realized this action was taken out of sheer delicacy. And she was very thankful to be left alone with her food. After all it was not so bad to be arrested, if all jail sentences were served in such nice clean kitchens, thought the girl.

But the reflection of a girl scout meeting at Flosston, and the stinging memory of the honor badge, picked up that night and carried off by the reckless Tessie, would torture her in spite of the more important issues in the girl's experience.

Where would Tessie go? Where would she stay and what would become of her? No doubt, as the officer had remarked, such a girl would easily become the prey of the unscrupulous, and at this thought Dagmar shuddered. What dreadful things always happen to runaway girls in the movies? Again the standard asserted its power.

Next moment the opening door announced Mrs. Cosgrove was back, and

Dagmar had "cleaned her plate."

"There now, you will feel better," and the woman quickly gathered up the tea dishes. "Come in the other room, and tell me your story before Jim comes back; sometimes a woman can help a girl more than a man can, and, as Jim says, I am sort of a wedge between the law and the victim," and she laughed lightly at the idea of interfering with her husband's business.

Dagmar told her story. She did not spare herself or attempt to cover her mistakes. She had left home because she was tired of Milltown and because she thought she would be better able to help her folks by getting out of the factory. Yes, she had listened to Tessie, and Tessie was different. Her mother allowed her out late nights, and had no objections to her going to dances in the factory hall, without brother or father. When Dagmar went her brother Frank always accompanied her.

"Well, that's encouraging," spoke Mrs. Cosgrove when Dagmar paused. "When folks have that much sense you can always talk to them. Now, when Molly comes we will talk it over with her. I wouldn't mind leaving off my work to-morrow, although I did plan to clean the cellar, and I could go out and see your mother—that is, if Molly thought there would be a chance for work for you here, and perhaps we could fix it so you could stay for a while anyway. I don't believe it would do you good to go right back in that crowd again. What you need is new chums."

"Oh, I couldn't give you all that trouble," objected Dagmar. "I am willing to go right back in the morning."

"It's right you should say so," continued the wise woman, "but you see, my girl, when you go back, you get right in the same rut again, and all those mill girls would just make life miserable for you. I am not encouraging you to stay away from home, but as Molly says, she is a leader in the scout girls you know—she always says when a thing goes wrong in one place it is best to try it in another. That is if the thing must be done, and, of course, you must work. However, wait until Molly comes in. She has learned so much since she has tried to teach others that I do believe she knows more than I do."

"You say she is a scout lieutenant?"

"Yes, they only take girls eighteen or over for that office and my Molly was eighteen two days before she was elected," and at the thought Mrs. Cosgrove indulged in a satisfactory chuckle.

It was all very bewildering to Dagmar, but just how it happened that she did not return to Flosston immediately was due to a very interesting plan made by Molly and co-operated in by her official father, and finally worked out by the near-official mother.

CHAPTER VI

A NOVEL JAIL

Thus it was that the girl scouts of Flosston and Lieutenant Molly Cosgrove of Franklin stumbled over the same case of a sister in need.

Returning from the big rally at the County Headquarters on that eventful evening, Molly Cosgrove found more than her usual hot cup of tea awaiting her. There was the strange young girl with the wonderful blue eyes, around which a telltale pink rim outlined the long silky lashes.

Molly thought she had never seen a prettier girl, while in turn Dagmar decided Molly Cosgrove was the very biggest, dearest, noblest girl she had ever seen. Formalities over, talk of the rally quickly put the stranger at ease.

"We had a wonderful rally," Molly enthused, "and at a business meeting held before the open session, it was decided to start obtaining recruits from the mills."

"Oh, that will be splendid!" exclaimed Dagmar, who now felt quite at home with the Cosgroves. "We have always wanted to know about those girl scouts."

"Well, you will soon have an opportunity," continued the girl, whose cheeks still glowed with rally excitement, "and I am a member of the committee appointed to visit the mills."

"That is just the thing," declared Mrs. Cosgrove, "for your boss always lets you follow the Troop orders, and by going into Flosston you may fix it for this scared little girl to stay here for a while."

"There, Mother, I always said you should be on the pay-roll. Isn't she the loveliest cop?" Molly asked Dagmar. "No wonder the Town Council thanked Mrs. Jim Cosgrove for her work among the women and girls! Why, Mom, you are a born welfare worker, and could easily have my position in the Mill. You see, I am what they call a welfare worker," again Molly addressed Dagmar directly.

38

"Oh, yes, I know. We have one in the Fluffdown Mill. Her name is Miss Mathews but she hardly ever comes in our room," offered Dagmar.

"Well, now Molly," said Mrs. Cosgrove very decidedly, "I just mentioned we might see that the girl got work in new surroundings, with you and me to keep an eye on her, so she could cut away from that crowd. What I have been able to find out is not much to its credit and there's reasons (with a look that pointed at Dagmar's beauty) why a girl like this should not run wild. It seems to me," smoothing out her big apron, by way of punctuation, "that it has all happened for the best. We can fix it so Pop won't make it an arrest after all, then you can get leave to go to Flosston first thing in the morning, can't you?"

"Oh, yes, the welfare work of all the big mills is co-related," replied the daughter, while the mother put her feet on the little velvet hassock, and seemed glad of the chance to draw her breath after the long speech.

Dagmar was sitting in one of the narrow arm chairs of the old- fashioned parlor suite. Her long, rather shapely hands traced the lines and cross-bars in her plaid skirt, and the sudden shifting of her gaze, from one speaker to the other, betrayed the nervousness she was laboring under.

"All right then, that's one more thing settled. And do you think the girl— say, girl, I don't like that name you have, what else can we call you?" she broke off suddenly with this question to Dagmar.

"My name is Dagmar Bosika, and I like Bosika best," replied the little stranger.

"All right, that's number three settled. You will be Bose. I can say that, but I never could think of the other queer foreign name."

"And we will have to change your last name, too, I guess," put in Molly, "as some one from Flosston might recognize it. We can just leave off the first syllable and have it Rose Dix or Dixon. I think Dixon would sound best."

"We are settling quite a few points," laughed Mrs. Cosgrove, "if some one doesn't upset them. I have no fears from Pop—"

"Oh, Pop is putty in our hands," went on the resourceful Molly, "no danger from his end. But how about your folks, Rose?"

Dagmar smiled before she replied. The new name struck on her ear a little oddly, but it pleased her, she had never liked Dagmar, and utterly despised the mill girls' nickname "Daggie."

"Mother and father have always said they would let me do what I thought would be best for me," she said at length. "I never did anything they told me I should not, and we often talked of my getting in a store or something like that. Mother works in the mill in another room, and she was always worried about me being away from her."

"A store would be no good for you," objected Mrs. Cosgrove, again including the girl's beauty in her scrutiny. "You would be best off within the reach of a welfare worker like Molly. But look at the time! Martin will be in from the club, and even Dad will be comin' around for his midnight coffee, before we call this meetin' to a halt. I say, Molly, we are runnin' an opposition scout meetin' it seems to me," and she got up with that finality, which plainly puts the period to all conversation.

A few moments later Rose had washed face and hands, brushed her hair, as Molly kindly hinted she should, and taking her shabby, washed, but unironed, night dress from the famous "telescope," she said her prayers and was ready for bed. How comfortable the room seemed! How strange she should be in it? And where was the unfortunate, headstrong Tessie?

A prayer for the safety of the wandering one sprung from the heart of this other girl, now away from home the very first night in her young life. That her mother would believe her at a girl's home, according to the little note left stuck in her looking glass, Rose was quite certain, so there was no need to worry concerning distress from the home circle, at least not yet, and tomorrow morning young Miss Cosgrove would go to the mill and very quietly arrange everything with her mother.

"The girl scouts are better than the police," she decided, not quite understanding how both could work so intimately, along different lines, yet each reaching the same result to assist wayward girls.

This was, surely, a queer sort of arrest, a lovely kind of cell, and a most friendly pair of jailers, the little runaway had fallen among, and that she dreamed wonderful dreams, glowing with roses and fragrant with perfume, was not to be wondered at, for Mrs. Cosgrove's linen was sweet enough to induce even more delicious fancies.

But what of poor, lost, erring, headstrong Tessie Warlitz? Rose imagined her in all sorts of wild predicaments, but with that kindness so marked in girls who have themselves suffered cruel misunderstandings, Rose determined not to betray her chum, but rather to do her utmost to find her, and win her back to good standing among girls—somehow. Thus really began in so subtle a manner her own interest in the principles of the Girl Scouts.

"To help an erring sister" is a fundamental of the cause, but Rose little knew what that silent consecration would cost her. When all was quiet, late that night, young Martin Cosgrove sauntered along home and giving the familiar "three dots and a dash" whistle notified his mother of his approach. The light in the sitting-room window had in its turn told Martin his mother awaited him.

"S-s-sh!" whispered the mother, opening the door very softly.

"Don't make any noise."

"What's up or who's sick?" asked the good-looking young man, pinching his mother's plump arm.

"There's a little girl asleep in the spare room. Don't wake her," cautioned the mother, who, to prevent even a hat falling, had secured Martin's things and was putting them on the rack.

"Friend of Molly's? Some new girl scout?" he asked, when they reached the seclusion of the kitchen.

"Well, no, not just that, but a poor child Dad found lost," she compromised.

"Lost, eh! And Chief of Police Mrs. Cosgrove rescued the lost chee-il-dd— as usual! Mom, you're a great cop, and I hear Molly is following in your fair footsteps!"

"Stop your nonsense, Marty, and be off to bed. It's awful late!

There's your fresh shirt for the morning. Take it along with you."

"Thanks, Mom, and you have the Chink beat in his line, too," giving the freshly ironed cambric shirt an approving pat. "Tell Molly to go easy out at Flosston. Those True Tred Girl Scouts are a pretty lively little bunch from what I hear."

"What do you mean?" asked the mother. "What did you hear about

Flosston?"

"Oh, just heard the boys talking. Nothing very much, but some girls ran away, not scouts, mill girls, mill detectives on their trail, and the Girl Scouts went on a hike and lassoed some poor guy by mistake. Oh, you know a lot of stuff like that, everybody hears and no one knows the real sense of. Only I thought Molly, just taking up with the Flosston work, ought to keep both eyes open, and wear good sensible shoes. Night, Mom!" and he kissed her very fondly. Mrs. Cosgrove indulged in two special brands of real pride—her boy and her girl!

CHAPTER VII

TENDERFOOT ADVENTURES

The ends of this story are winding out like the strings of a Maypole, and just like those pretty dancing streamers, do the story lines all swing from the pole of the Girl Scout activities.

The Flosston rally was held for the purpose of planning a broader program, and as told by Lieutenant Cosgrove, the arrangements there were made to afford the mill girls a chance to enjoy the meetings, and to participate generally in the regular membership. These plans had already thrown their influence over an entire chain of the big factories of Eastern Pennsylvania.

Most of the plants employed one or two women welfare workers in their ranks, following the campaign waged by progressive women in the interests of better conditions among women wage-earners. This qualification pertained to girls as well as adults.

So it was that young Molly Cosgrove, an assistant welfare worker, would be allowed to go from one mill to another in carrying out the new movement of Girl Scouts for mill workers between the ages of sixteen and twenty-two years. No girl under sixteen was supposed to be at work in mills, and if any such was found she must have been listed at the required minimum, sixteen.

The sensational news of two girls having run away from the Fluffdown mills was now quickly making its way through Flosston and near-by communities. The Wartliz family had done its part in spreading the scandal, while the Brodix people said little, wagged their heads and grieved sincerely, for their Dagmar was a cherished daughter, and her loss had sadly strained the humble home circle.

The fact that Miss Cosgrove had arrived at Fluffdown and talked with Mrs. Brodix was known only to those workers directly at that particular bench, and they quickly surmised the welfare worker was making inquiries about Dagmar.

Instead, she had brought to the alarmed mother the news of her daughter's safety and secretly a plan had been made, whereby this little black-eyed woman would soon come out to Franklin on an evening, to see Dagmar, now known as Rose, and so make sure that the kind offices of the new found friends would be thoroughly understood, and likewise agreed to by Mrs. Brodix.

Not even the talkative Kate Jordan, who worked next to Mrs. Brodix and kept her eyes and ears attentive during Molly Cosgrove's visit to the afflicted mill hand, guessed any of this, while the escape of Tessie Wartliz, from the very grasp of Officer Cosgrove, remained a secret with those who directly encountered the business end of that experience.

Meanwhile the girls of True Tred were radiant with the prospect of their work—that of assisting the mill girls and actually taking part in real Americanization. To the younger girls, especially Cleo, Grace and Madaline, the plan opened a field of exciting adventure, for they had never been allowed to visit the mills, and were not encouraged to make acquaintance among the workers.

"Now," said Cleo, when the three Tenderfoots got together after school was dismissed, "we will have as much real fun with live girls as we have ever seen played out in the pictures. Some mill girls do the queerest things, talk so funny, you can scarcely understand them, and they act—well, just like a play. Florence Hayden says so, she helped with their Christmas Sunday School entertainment last year."

"Oh, well," demurred Madaline more kindly, "they never went to our schools. Some of them went to the Town Hall night school, but they only met their friends there and never got a chance to learn our ways."

"You're a real good little home missionary, Madie," commented Grace, "and I'll vote for you when the mill committees are made up, only," and she puckered her pretty mouth into a rosette intended to express deep scorn, "of course we're too young, and we are only in the Tenderfoot Class."

"I suppose Margaret will be picked," said Cleo, "she is fifteen and first class and has had a merit badge."

"But she lost it," Grace reminded the trio.

"And is going to get another from headquarters, Captain Clark said so."

"Well, she deserves it, I'm sure," protested Cleo.

"Oh, of course she does, but I would, too, if my plan worked out the other day," went on Grace.

"What plan?" demanded Cleo, while Madaline pulled a long, serious face.

"Oh, I wanted to do something noble and I tried to, but it did not just work out," faltered Grace, "but—I—am going—to try it again!" and her eyes blazed defiance at Madaline.

"You just do, Grace Philow, and I'll—"

"Who cares!" interrupted the unconquerable Grace, while Cleo looked a whole volume of inquiries.

The McKay twins were romping over from a near-by playhouse, a little tepee made of cast off "shutters" the janitor had put outside after wrenching them from hinges, and the girls had promptly availed themselves of the material for a most attractive playhouse.

"Hello! hello!" called both. "Who wants a ride home? Mother is sending the big car."

"Oh, we all do, of course," spoke Cleo, the first to mingle words with her delight. "Who wouldn't love a ride in that big, spiffy limousine!"

"Well, thank you just the same, but I don't, just today," Grace surprised them with answering. "I have an appointment with Brother Benny."

"Oh!" said Winnie McKay significantly.

"I see!" drawled her sister Norma.

"Suit yourself," deprecated Cleo.

"If you can't, you can't," philosophized Madaline.

"That's exactly it," amplified Grace. "I can't, so I can't. Thank you, Winnie and Norma, for the lovely invitation, and please let me put it down to my credit account? I would like a refund," and she laughed her irresistible explosive outburst, in which the whole party joined, whether willingly or from acute inflection.

A few moments later the party, all but Grace, climbed into the lovely, softly lined car, and when Winnie told the chauffeur to drive to the post-office first, Cleo was delighted to find she had a postal card to drop in the box. That would give every one around the Green a chance to see the style of the McKay twins and their school chums.

And while the big car rolled smoothly over Oakley Avenue, Grace and Bennie were hurrying about — over a woodland road too rough and too narrow for other traffic than just nimble, willing feet.

"You're crazy!" declared Benny, halting at the prospect of the long winding path Grace led him to, and insisted was the "right way."

"That's what the girls say," answered the sister, "but really, Benny, I am not at all. Just as sane as — Libby Lintot, and you know every one says she is as crazy as a loon. But all the same if we follow this path we will come to my tree, and maybe we will find a lovely dead tramp all buried in the spring pine needles, tied up by Grace Philow Tenderfoot!"

"Grace Philow lunatic!" answered the brother. "Nice thing to make a fellow miss a whole afternoon on marbles, just to hunt a tied-up tramp!"

"Would you rather hunt tigers'?" asked Grace, running along like a wild squirrel, jumping over rocks and springing across the perpetual little streams and brooklets.

"Sure I would, wouldn't you? What's an old tramp?" sneered Bennie.

"Wait till you see him," promised Grace, "he's lovely. That is I think he is. I didn't exactly see his face, I was so busy tieing him up," explained the sister.

Benny, two years younger than Grace, went forth on the man hunt, armed with his pop gun and water pistol. It was actually two days after the eventful experience of Grace and Madaline in River Bend Wood, when the latter had made such a desperate attempt to rescue the alleged "Mrs. Johnston's wash," but though many hours had passed, Grace was still haunted with the awful possibilities of her beloved tramp dying there, all tied up with clove hitches and running bowlines, while the birds scattered spring blossoms over his handsome face. True, she had hoped today, on this second expedition, to recover the lost wash, but to get to that big tree, and relieve the gnawing anxiety, was her first determination; dead or alive she must have a look at the tramp! Nothing could be worse than this awful uncertainty!

"That's the grove over there! See the big straight tree! That's my tree!" she exclaimed, dragging along the erstwhile brave Benny, who just now showed an inclination to come to a full stop. "Come on, Benny, hold on to me. I'll peek first, from the other big tree back of the ivy stump. Then we can see without being seen."

Like a pair of chipmunks they hopped from tree to tree, being careful to keep well in the shadow of one before risking a new position behind another.

"Just like shadow tag," Benny made chance to whisper. "Gee, Sis, this is some little scouting."

"Better than your Boy Scouts' games, isn't it, Benny?" Grace apologized, for indeed it was no easy matter to inveigle the big boy into a little girl's sport. Benny felt much bigger, and decidedly more mature than Grace—that is, he felt that way.

47

"Oh, Ben, see!" exclaimed the sister. "There's something flying- over — maybe over a grave!"

"Swell chance he had to — make — his own grave!" in contemptuous tones from Benny.

"Well — it is a red flag, flying over something!" Grace whispered emphatically.

Benny sprang out from his tree and with one hand on the automatic-loaded water pistol, and the other on the lead-loaded pop gun, he confronted the hypothetical grave!

"Come on out, Sis," he invited the frightened Grace. "It isn't no grave. It's just a red handkerchief on a stick."

Glancing furtively in the direction of the road, which ran parallel with the river path, and near enough to it to carry a voice from the woods to the road should emergency demand outcry, Grace stepped very gingerly out from her hiding into the open space in front of the famous "inhabited" tree.

Yes, there was the red flag! "Wasn't that a signal for war? The flag was a red handkerchief, and it swayed from a stick cut from a variegated birch.

"Oh!" sighed Grace, relief and excitement finding an outlet in that short syllable.

"Look at the signal!" called Benny, now going straight up boldly to the flag of fury. "See, it's a wig-wag, pointing to that big rock. Let's look!" and be followed the pointing stick which, tied to the top of the improvised flagpole plainly meant — due west — to any one who understood the scout wig-wag code. "Here!" shouted Benny, now casting caution to the light winds of murmuring pines. "Here's more trail. See? It's our secret code of turned over sliver leaves, and it leads to — let's see." Benny was visibly excited and Grace was almost pulling him down from the rock in her eagerness to follow the signs. He turned over a rock which showed loose soil, and dried leaves clinging to its jagged sides. "Here it is, Grace! Sure enough! Here is a letter from your dead tramp. Maybe he died right after he wrote it," and even the small boy found humor in the queer uncanny situation.

"Take it out by the roadway," suggested Grace, to whom the woods were now a little treacherous. She glared at as many trees as two brown eyes could embrace. "We can read it out under the big maple. Come on, Benny," she begged, dragging him forth again away from all the woodland mysteries.

CHAPTER VIII

CLUE TO THE MISSING

So many and such exciting sequels are divulged through helpless little letters! How innocently the page of paper carries the silent words, yet how powerful is the influence to cheer or sadden!

Grace had read her mystic letter, but beyond confiding in Benny, whose word of honor in secrecy she had exacted, not one single syllable of that note was to be divulged to any one.

She had hopes that something really wonderful would develop from her remarkable experience, and while she would have liked to tell Madaline and Cleo, she feared antagonistic opinions, and, as it was entirely her own personal secret, and not a matter of girl scout business, or even chums' interest, it seemed decidedly better to keep her own precious counsel.

"I'll tell them all when it happens!" she assured herself, by no means being certain just what she hoped "would happen."

So the mystic letter was tucked away in the tiny, pink silk vanity bag, which Cleo had given Grace the Christmas before, and in the days following only her starry eyes threatened to betray the interesting fact, that the little Tenderfoot harbored a dark, delicious secret.

Meanwhile Rose had taken her place in the Franklin mill and was being cared for by the benevolent Mrs. Cosgrove as a member of her family.

"It was really providential," Molly told her mother one day at lunch, after having seen for the second time the parents of Dagmar Brodix, "for the family had to leave Pennsylvania, and it would have been very hard for them to take Rose along. It seems Mr. Brodix would not join the union, and both he and his wife had to be discharged to appease the labor men. Rose, too, would have been ordered out, as the whole family come under the ban imposed on the father."

"Poor folks!" deplored Mrs. Cosgrove. "Those unions won't let anybody think for themselves! Where are they going?"

"Away down east to a big silk mill," replied the daughter. "Mr. Brodix knew the superintendent in his own country, and got in the shop without a union card. But it is much better for Rose to stay with us until they get settled at least."

"I took such a fancy to that child the moment I set eyes on her!"

Mrs. Cosgrove explained to Molly.

"You always do, Mumsey!" laughed the daughter, "but I entirely agree with you this time. Where is Rose now?"

"Just gone to the post-office. She came in at twelve and finished her dinner in time for a bit of fresh air before going back. How is she getting on in her work?"

"First rate, the forelady reports. Rose is naturally quiet, and as you predict, Mother, it is very important for her to be among new companions. A girl's pretty face is not always a help to her best interests."

"Exactly, Molly. Everybody seems to pick on a pretty girl, while they leave the homely ones to tend their own business. But your dad is much worried about that other damsel who got away. There is no trace of her at all."

"Yes, she made a clear escape. I heard one of the mill detectives making some inquiries. He did not have to question Rose. I gave him our end of it. I am afraid that other girl has gotten herself into more trouble. The detective did not say so outright, but I judged so from his line of questions."

"Your father said as much, but like the detective, our own 'cop' isn't giving us all the information he holds. I'm glad the mill officials see the value of the girl scout movement. It's the only fair way to reach the girls without forcing them. Let them take a hand in their own interest—I always say."

"The mill men see the wisdom of that. I would not have been

51

engaged as a welfare worker if I had not been a scout lieutenant.

Well, I must run along. We have a meeting in Flosston tonight, and I am going to take Rose with me."

"I would. The girls of the troop have never met her to know her, and, at any rate, their training will check any possible criticism. Good-bye, girl. Better take your umbrella. We will have rain before sunset," and with this word mother and daughter separated for their respective afternoon tasks.

Meanwhile Rose had called at the post-office. Her anxiety concerning the wayward Tessie constituted the one flaw in her otherwise happy new days. That she could not at once be with her parents was clear and reasonable to the girl, reared in hardship, and accustomed to many personal sacrifices, but that an incriminating letter would surely one day come from Tessie kept her nervously anxious.

Rose had contrived to visit the post-office daily, hoping when the dreaded, yet longed-for, letter would come, she might receive it personally and thus avert possible complications with the Cosgrove family, who had official reasons for wishing to locate the runaway girl.

With that keenness peculiar to foreigners when a matter vitally concerns them, the Brodix people had readily adopted the more useful name Dixon for their daughter, and today, when Rose inquired for mail, a much-soiled letter addressed to "Rose Dixon, care of Mrs. James Cosgrove," was handed out.

Not risking the publicity of opening the envelope until she was well out of sight of observers, Rose hurried along, and turned an unnecessary corner to seclude herself in a particularly quiet street, there to open and read the letter. Somehow she felt it would contain news of Tessie, and her premonition was correct.

"From mother!" she breathed affectionately, as the much handled little sheet of note paper, with its queer foreign script, lay in her hand. Then she noticed an inclosure. Yes! There was the note from Tessie!

So anxious was Rose to know where Tessie was, she glimpsed through the little note without actually reading one word of it. She was just looking for a clue as to the girl's whereabouts, but to her disappointment none was given! Not one word showed the capital letter at its face, that would have marked the name of any place! Tessie wrote English well enough to make herself understood, and the brief note was almost explosive in its choice of strong phrases. The "quarter whistle" blew, announcing to Rose the fact that fifteen minutes of the precious noon hour still remained, and as ten would be ample time for her to reach the mill, in the five extra minutes she might read her letters.

Stopping at a little stone wall, which surrounded one of the oldest houses in Franklin, Rose read first the note from Tessie. As she expected, the "news" was more a compilation of strong slang than an attempt to impart any real information, and although but a short time removed from the acute influence of "chewing-gum English," Rose had already developed a dislike for the more vulgar of such forms of utterance. She read:

"Hello, kid! Where are you? Did you break loose from Grandpa? I had some beatin' to do, but I done it and made a get-a-way good 'nough for the movies. Don't ask me where I'm at, for it's a secret. But, say, Kid. Oh, you scout badge! It's a miracle worker— and better than real coin. I wouldn't give it up for a Liberty Bond. So long! can't tell you just now what my private post-office box is but will later. My folks are cross-eyed looking for me, but all they ever wanted was my pay-envelope, so I should worry about them. Give my love to yourself and if you're not out of jail yet for the love of molasses, don't be a simp! Get busy!" It was signed "T. W."

And that was all; so like Tessie. Rose sighed audibly, then read her mother's letter and while this was really interesting to the daughter it now seemed tame in comparison, and it really was the letter from Tessie that gave her blue eyes the preoccupied look all that afternoon.

So the lost and found scout badge was serving the runaway girl as a passport. Perhaps she was using it for unworthy purposes, and it was unlawful to wear a scout badge without authority. The offence was punishable by law. Rose thoroughly understood all this, but how could she reach Tessie to warn her! Even a dismissed scout must return her badge and buttons to the organization, and there was Tessie Wartliz forging her way on the strength of that special merit badge!

Such thoughts as these riveted the attention of Rose, when Molly Cosgrove, passing through the room, whispered she could go with the lieutenant to the Flosston meeting that night.

"All right. Thank you!" replied Rose to the invitation, but, somehow, she dreaded its acceptance.

CHAPTER IX

A TRIBUTE OF ROSES

The little meeting room over the post-office in Flosston had served as headquarters for True Tred Troop—and tonight Margaret Slowden was to receive her new badge, to take the place of that much-prized little gilt wreath with its clover leaf center, her merit badge lost some weeks before.

"Hurry along!" called Grace, who was impatiently waiting for Cleo and Madaline, both of whom seemed to enjoy lagging while Grace wanted to be early rather than late. "Don't you know we have to take our tests and Captain Clark ordered us to be at headquarters at seven-fifteen sharp?"

"All right," responded Cleo, "but here come Mable Blake and Mildred Clark. We can all be together if you just wait half a second for us, Grace."

"I don't mind seconds, but I hate hours!" retorted Grace. "I don't want to be a moment late and give anyone a chance to think up hard questions for my tests."

"Oh, you needn't worry," Cleo assured her. "I know you can beat us all at knots."

That brought back to Grace her attempt to make a "clove-hitch" and a "running bowline carry out her noble deed" and she flashed a significant look at Madaline, who shared a part of her secret.

"Oh, yes, I know the knots," she replied. "But you just ought to see me try to light my fire in the open, with two matches! More like two boxes I guess."

"And my simple dish," contributed Mildred Clark, who now, with her companions, had joined the group, and all were merrily making their way to the meeting room. "I thought I would select the very simplest of the simple, and I took pork and beans."

"You did!" exclaimed a chorus.

"Yes, and it is a real wonder I am here. I thought I never would get out of that old hot kitchen. Martha told me I should have taken Irish stew but—"

"But you preferred the Boston Bake," interrupted Mable Blake.

"Of course Mildred wouldn't have anything to do with the Irish!" teased Madaline, who was well known to have "leanings" in that direction.

"Indeed, I will never scorn the Celts again!" sighed Mildred, "for I had to brown the pork and it burned. I had to soak the beans all night and they swelled up so I had to scoop them up on a dust pan next morning. I didn't use those, of course," as the girls' looks protested, "I had enough on the floor to plant a garden and I really did plant them. Then, the big pan full I baked, and it took all day. Did you ever know plain pork and beans constituted an exact science in the preparation for the table? Why didn't I try milk toast, and get finished in time for your ball game, girls? Don't you think I am a real hero of the simple dish-pork and beans?"

"We surely do, Millie, and I hope you get a perfect mark for all that work," spoke up Grace. "My real trouble came in making a bed. That sounds so easy, but our beds have lace covers, and no sooner would I get one end straight, than the other would be all draped up in little cascades. Don't you all just hate to make beds?"

"Oh, no, I love to do it," declared Mabel. "But just let me show you my flag. Doesn't it look like a crazy quilt design?" and from her scout manual she unfolded a page of paper, with the required American flag drawn and colored in crayons, and not really a poor illustration of her beloved Old Glory.

"Well, you have all had your troubles, but I think mine was by far the most complicated and exasperating," Cleo declared, coherent conversation being made quite possible by the double file in which the girls grouped themselves, as they walked along. "You should just see me take my measurements. Of course I forgot to follow instructions and 'see card at headquarters,' as the little blue book directs."

"My sakes!" exclaimed Grace. "Do we have to have our measurements tonight?"

"We must answer all test questions and that is one of them," replied Cleo. "But when I got my height by using a pencil over my head on a door-post, of course we all do that, I had a set of cords all knotted up at points to show waist, chest, arm, etc., and our pet kitten, Cadusolus, made a tackle for the whole bunch, and before I could recover them she had taken her own measures on my marked strings. I won't be sure of them now, for I had to finish them in a big hurry after that."

"I know the Mariner's Compass by heart," called in Mabel Blake from the rear line. "Brother Jack tested me, and he said I could sail an ocean liner with my knowledge," she insisted proudly.

"We have our tests first, don't we?" asked Grace.

"Yes, of course, that all happens outside in the private troop room, but I'll bet the other girls listen at the keyhole!" put in Mildred.

"And last time a lot of boys on the back fence could see in the window," Madaline reminded the anxious aspirants.

"Oh, there go all the other girls, let's hurry," urged Cleo, and when the candidates mounted the stairs over the post-office, they were but a small part of the noisy crowd that pounded its way on the narrow and rather uncertain steps.

All of the officers assisted in the examinations so that not more than a half hour was consumed in that detail, and when the girls filed into the drill room, their smiling faces announced the good news that all had passed.

Quickly at the given signal all the troops "fell in" and the regulation "horse shoe" was formed with Captain Clark and Lieutenant Lindsley in the gap, when the salute was given and the other formalities complied with and each candidate was conducted to the captain. After answering the captain's questions and saluting, each candidate received her staff, neckerchief and knot from the patrol leader, while the badge was pinned on the blouse of the solemn-faced girls by the captain herself.

All of this was conducted with a striking degree of seriousness, and as the exercises made Tenderfoots out of the newest candidates, our own little friends looked on, with united dignity, while they awaited their turn to receive degrees of the second and first class.

The tests for Tenderfoot were but simple, and consisted mainly of knots made and the knowledge of scout laws, with a few civic questions, so that the beginners shared no part of the anxiety experienced by Cleo, Grace and Madaline, and those of their higher grades. The distinction of advancement is the privilege of wearing the badge on the left sleeve, second class below the elbow and first class above on the same arm, so that ceremonial occupied but a brief space of time.

No conversation was permitted during the Investure, but the presence of Rose, who sat in a corner looking on with wondering eyes, had not been unobserved by the scouts. That she had come from Franklin with Lieutenant Cosgrove was sufficient credential for the privilege of being present during the ceremonial, but it was Grace who talked with her eyes to Cleo, directing her interpretative glances from the pretty little stranger, to the now duly installed second-class scout, her message being, "See that pretty strange girl over there?" and Cleo replying in turn with her glance, "Yes, isn't she pretty? Who is she?"

With all her light-heartedness, which was sometimes termed "light-headedness," Grace was fast developing a new sense, somewhat related to our old friend Common Sense. Ever since she tried her girl scout knot in the woods, and had eventually received a real letter from the actual victim, she had been planning to "confess" to the other girls, and seek their advice. First, she made up her mind to tell Madaline, as that friend already knew a part of the secret, but the fact that Cleo was credited with better judgment swayed her toward that counsel. Then came such a succession of busy days, busy afternoons and busy evenings, Grace could find no available time for the portentous, confidential conventions of chums. So no one but Benny had, as yet, heard anything of the mysterious letter found in the holly rock in River Bend Woods.

But this evening during all the scout ceremony Grace and her conscience were having a silent battle on the score of the prolonged secrecy. Grace wished to wait a little while longer but her conscience fought for immediate confession. Only the importance of Captain Clark's speech seemed sufficiently strong to drag her attention from this mental conflict.

"In striving for honors," the captain was now stating, "Girl Scouts must be careful to use prudence and wisdom. It will not do to rush into personal danger to do something that may seem to be brave and noble, when a less hazardous means of accomplishing the same end may be found, if intelligently sought for."

Grace sank back in her seat. The captain's eyes seemed to be directed straight at her! Could anyone have told Captain Clark?

"All our special honor and merit badges are tokens of noble deeds, done for humanity according to the principles laid down by our rules, and explained in our manual, but none of these should be interpreted as involving unnecessary risk to us, or the use of our guns, our ropes, our staffs in any violence which might be avoided!"

"Ropes!" repeated Grace under her breath. "We should not—use—our ropes—"

"Grace!" whispered Madaline. "See that big bunch of roses over there!"

"Yes!" nodded Grace.

"They are for Margaret Slowden when she gets her new merit badge, and nobody knows who sent them!"

"Uh-hum-m!" breathed Grace in assent.

When Captain Clark finished her practical talk, the ceremony of bestowing the substitute badge on Margaret was the nest feature of the evening's exercises.

"You all recall our lovely ceremony on the evening of Margaret's original presentation of her merit badge," the captain said, "but this time we have merely to call attention to that great occasion and our minds are filled with its pleasant memories. The noble deed done to acquire this badge was one of unusual heroism and peculiar wisdom," she went on, "for Margaret stayed at her post in a dreary, lonely room, guarding her hats and cloaks with the same spirit of attention to duty which at that same hour was bringing her distinguished brother his consecrated D.S.C. We will now pin upon Margaret's breast—a badge to take the place of that one, lost some time ago, and we all hope she will be doubly rewarded by the second badge of merit!"

There was a stir in the audience and Margaret was conducted to the platform by her patrol leader. Captain Clark then pinned on her coat the new badge, with the words of commendation, and this concluded, an usher advanced with the bouquet. The captain glanced at the card before indicating that the testimonial be presented. It was inscribed merely—"A Friend."

Everyone was puzzled. It was very unusual to give hot-house flowers in May. Then a side door was heard to creak on its hinges and the pretty stranger, Rose Dixon, was just seen passing out.

"I wonder why she left?" Madaline asked Grace.

"Oh, I don't know, but I would like to leave myself," unexpectedly retorted Grace.

"Sick?" persisted Madaline.

"No—just tired," and no one knew better than Grace what a conscience prodder such a meeting as this proved to be—that is "no one" except, perhaps, Rose Dixon.

CHAPTER X

TELLING SECRETS

Determined to wait no longer than the very next afternoon, Grace asked both Cleo and Madaline over to her front porch directly after school, assuring their acceptance to her invitation by the lure of "a big secret to tell them." Needless to say, they came, and there, in the shadow of the yellow and white honeysuckle blossoms, with busy bees buzzing in and out of the honey-filled cups, Grace disclosed the story of her second trip to River Bend Woods.

The girls were fascinated. To think the tied-up man had written a letter!

"Yes, but," argued Grace. "I am a little timid ever since. See, he says he hopes he can lasso me some day with my own rope! Just suppose he does!"

"Oh, I am sure he was just joking there," wise little Cleo ventured. "He just said that to tease you, for teasing him."

"Maybe," replied Grace rather tonelessly.

"Let me see it again," begged Madaline, reaching for the well- fingered little sheet of paper. "But he says," she read, "he liked your courage, and he hated to spoil all your nice scout knots. That must mean he is a good friend."

"Oh, it might just mean the opposite," gloomed Grace, who had read the letter so many times every syllable weighed a clause to her. "He may have meant that merely in sarcasm."

"Who ever do you suppose he was?" asked Madaline foolishly.

"Is, you mean," corrected Grace. "He didn't die, so he still is."

"Of course, that's what I mean. Only he isn't there now, so he was, I think," insisted Madaline, without taking any offence at the crispness of Grace's manner.

"Whether he is or whether he was, we might get along better if we tried to guess who he could possibly be," Cleo assisted. "Have you the least idea?"

"Not the slightest. You see, that sheet of paper came out of a notebook, and anyone could own a notebook or even find one," Grace speculated.

"Let me read the whole letter through?" asked Cleo. "We can't make sense out of single sentences."

Grace handed over the much-criticized little missive. She read aloud:

"LITTLE SCOUT BANDIT:

"I hate to spoil all your pretty knots, but I can't stay tied up any longer. I am taking the rope along, and some day I hope to lasso you in return. You gave me a merry chase after my bag — quite a little runner you are. When I chance this way again I will look for an answer in our hollow rock. Good luck, Scout Bandit —

"THE VICTIM."

"There!" exclaimed Madaline, "only an educated man could write that!"

"But many wicked men are wonderfully educated!" Grace insisted on worrying.

"He seems jolly," mused Cleo.

"All tramps joke," said Grace.

"Well, if you want a tramp, have one," laughed Cleo. "We won't mind, Gracie."

"I'm not Gracie, and I hate tramps. I tried to be nice to one when I was a little girl. Mother was giving him pie and coffee, and I said it was hard for men to be tramps. He turned right around and hissed: 'You're too gabby!' That's the way tramps appreciate kindness."

"And you called him a tramp to his face!" exclaimed Madaline.

"Oh, girls, leave the old tramp alone and let's get to the new wild-westerner," begged Cleo. "I'll tell you what we'll do. Let's write an answer to his letter, and explain we only wanted to do something brave for our Scout honors, but we understand better now, and Grace, do you want to say you're sorry you tied him up?"

"No, indeed I do not!" snapped Grace. "Why should I, when I was trying to get Mrs. Johnston's wash!"

"Oh, Cleo doesn't know about that," Madaline reminded Grace. "We forgot that. You see, Cleo," she continued, "the man had a bag of clothes beside him, and Grace got a hook made of a good strong stick. She tied this to her rope (she had a lot of ropes with her to practice her knots, you know), but when she saw the bag, and thought she saw things like Mrs. Johnston's wash, why, of course, she just tried to get it."

"And I did, too," insisted Grace, "I dragged it all the way to the big rock. Then we heard some one coming, but I held fast, I never lost it until the bag got stuck behind the rock. I wanted so much to get poor Mrs. Johnston's wash," she lamented.

"Well, shall we write the letter?" Cleo followed up.

"I have to say I am afraid to go in the woods now," admitted

Grace. "Suppose he should capture us all!"

"We could make some excuse to bring a lot of girls along,"

Madeline suggested. "He couldn't capture a whole troop."

"Wouldn't it be better to get some big strong boy to fetch the letter out there for us?" proposed the practical Cleo.

"Whom could we trust?" Grace asked.

"I wouldn't depend on brothers. They are too tricky. But how about Hal Crane? He is always interested in our troop doings, and besides he's a good scout himself. I think I would ask him," Cleo determined.

"All right," agreed Grace, "and Cleo dear," with her arms around the girl at the end of the bench, "won't you be a darling and write the letter?"

"And get lassoed?" laughed her chum. "Well, I don't mind. I think he must be a very nice man, and maybe I shall adopt him for my hero."

"You may. I would be very glad to get rid of him," Grace confessed. "I was so worried all this time, and I couldn't get a chance to tell you a word about it."

"And I can imagine every rope you saw you just imagined was coming your way," teased Cleo.

"Just about. But say, girls, another thing. Did you see that pretty girl who came in last night with the lieutenant from Franklin?"

"Oh, yes, the pretty blonde with the blue crocheted tam, I saw her. I guess everyone did," Madaline replied.

"Well, she was so pretty I couldn't help watching her, and I am sure she acted awfully nervous when the flowers were sent up to Margaret."

"She went out directly the ushers took up the bouquet," Madaline added. "And never came back for the ice cream," went on Grace. "Well, what I wanted to say is, I have seen that pretty girl before and I sort of think she was the one who used to be with the dark-eyed girl they say ran away."

"Why, she came with Lieutenant Cosgrove, and surely wouldn't be a companion to a runaway mill girl!" protested Madaline.

"You forget, newly second class, that we are taking in the mill girls in our troop, and are all pledged to do our best to help them," Grace declared. "I know more than one very nice girl in Fluffdown. Daddy is one of the superintendents there."

"Yes, of course," Cleo acquiesced. "And my daddy is in charge of the main office."

"I am sure we should be interested in that line, and our scouting is so practical. I understand Lieutenant Lindsley is going to call a special meeting of True Tred to make definite plans. Some of our girls need education in social latitude, quite as much as do the mill girls, she told us last night, and, judging from the way Hattie Thompson laughed when a mill girl slipped in the mud the other day, I think some of the girls need a special course in common politeness," said Madaline.

"There come Ben's boys," Grace announced. "Let's go out on the lawn and have a game of 'Heel and Toe.'"

"I can't, Grace. I have some shopping to do for mamma, and we have been talking nearly an hour," Cleo declared, glancing at her wrist watch. "You stay, Madaline. Don't go because I have to."

"I really must go," Madaline also insisted. "But be sure, Grace, that Cleo understands all about the letter," she added.

"I will write it and call a meeting of this committee to consider it," proposed Cleo. "Isn't it lovely and exciting?"

"You may think so, but I am glad I no longer have to lug that secret around all alone," said Grace, as the girls were preparing to leave.

"Almost as heavy as Mrs. Johnston's wash," teased Madaline. "Well, good-bye, Grace. We will do all we can to find — you know."

Benny was almost close enough to hear the parting words, but in his boyish head, chuck full of sports and frolics, he had little room for girls' secrets, and even the knowledge thrust upon him by Grace in her trip to the woods had long ago gone the way of his lost game of "Bear in the Pit." Boys have a wonderful way of forgetting failures, and it is that trait which later entitles them to the claims of being good sports, using the title "sport" in its best and most vigorous application.

"Well, that's over, thank goodness!" breathed Grace, referring to her "confession," as she smilingly turned to her piano practice, a duty indifferently done since her encounter with the writer of the mysterious letter.

CHAPTER XI

THE TANGLED WEB

While the Girl Scouts of Flosston were arranging to extend their troop activities so that they would include the girls from Fluffdown mills, who wished to join, two other girls were becoming more and more involved in an influence, seemingly subtle, but surely sufficiently powerful to "win out" eventually.

Tessie Wartliz was enmeshed in that oftquoted "tangled web," coincident with the first attempt at deception.

"Oh, what a tangled web we weave When first we practice to deceive!"

Reading those lines mean very little to the girl who has never been so unfortunate as to know their fullest meaning, but Tessie knew not the lines, it was their threat she felt, their dark story she was living through.

Rose returned from the rally of the True Tred Troop with deeper blue in her eyes and brighter pink in her cheeks. It had been so wonderful! To see all those girls promising to do so much, not only for one another, but for all girls, then the inspiring ceremony, the lovely exercises, the music! It did not seem possible that all this came to the good fortune of some girls in that mill town, while others struggled to gain advantage over their companions, as they worked in gloomy surroundings, prone to some sort of rebellion.

And to think Rose had been asked to help carry this new story to her former companions, and to those with whom she was now associated!

Sitting for a few precious moments in her little room at Mrs. Cosgrove's, although her light had been extinguished, and it was too late to enjoy the tempting reverie, Rose, even in the dark, could feel the comfort and sense the luxury of that simple, well- ordered home. How strange that she should have been picked up from the peril of waywardness, and become so safely sheltered by these benevolent strangers! Was it because Molly Cosgrove, too, taught and practiced the girl scout principles, and because Mrs. Cosgrove was a pioneer from whom such principles emanate?

Gradually Rose sensed the difference in American and foreign ideals, and now it was as if the curtain had lifted, and her own mind was cleared of the confusing doubts and suspicions she had heretofore struggled with.

The soft, sweet air of young summer wafted from the flowery vines, caressed her pretty face as she stared out of the low window into the velvet night, and she was glad, so glad she had sent those roses!

"If only I could have returned that badge!" she pondered; "why did

Tessie run off with it!"

The dark thought immediately cast a shadow over her happiness just at that moment, a vagrant cloud in a sky almost untarnished, deliberately sailed into the moon, and blackened the window through which Rose gazed.

"I guess that means bed!" she decided and promptly slipped between the grateful covers. But not to sleep. The thoughts of Tessie and her insinuating letters were too persistent to be immediately banished. Try as she might, Rose could find no key to the problem of how to reach the girl and reclaim the innocent badge, now serving as a baneful influence in the uncertain career of Tessie Wartliz.

"If only I could talk with her just a few minutes," Rose kept repeating, and that wish became the source of a plan, from which sprung a new resolve.

She must see Tessie!

Fixed in her brain, that resolve actually took root, and even in sleep it seemed to grow, to get stronger with the hours, and to mature with courage silently imparted through tired nature's sweet restorer. Balmy sleep!

Troubled dreams discovered the runaway girl in strange surroundings, now working in a dark gloomy mill, and flashing her black eyes like lighted coals at every word of correction offered by her superiors, again

Tessie seemed to be enjoying the soft luxury of some favored home, a wild flower in a garden of hot- house blooms.

But it was all a dream, and Rose knew nothing of Tessie's adventure, beyond the suspicions conveyed in the two sketchy letters sent since the escapade.

A few days later the Leader, an evening paper, contained a story startling to the girls of Flosston, and positively shocking to Rose Dixon. This told of a young girl claiming to be a girl scout, running off with a lot of ticket money, the funds she had obtained by pretending to assist an entertainment being conducted for the benefit of the Violet Circle of Shut-ins.

That a girl scout should rob cripples! And that a clue should lead back to Flosston, inferring the culprit might belong in that town! Instantly Rose knew the mystery meant Tessie, and that the purloined badge had served as her scout credential!

Panic seized her! She had seen the paper on her way home from work, and at table, when Molly Cosgrove discussed the item, Rose felt her own guilt must be obvious to those around her. Yet no one knew Tessie had taken the badge. No one knew Rose had found the pretty emblem!

"How could a girl scout act so dishonorably?" Molly questioned indignantly.

"And she actually got away with the money," Mrs. Cosgrove repeated. "Some young bold girls can cover their tracks better than hardened men."

Rose felt her cheeks pale. She had never known the antics of nervous chill, but just now a series of "goose-flesh-flashes" chased all over her.

"You must be very tired, Rose," remarked Molly keenly. "Better go to bed early and omit the meeting. Mrs. Brennen, the welfare leader at Conit, is coming over, but you can hear her another time. You had nervous work on those scarfs to-day. I heard the girls say that floss stuck like chiffon."

"It was sticky," Rose was glad to comment, "and I guess I won't go over to the school house if you don't mind. Perhaps I will just take a walk in the air and later write a few letters."

"The fresh air is what you want," Mrs. Cosgrove unconsciously assisted in the plans seething through the troubled brain of Rose. "I've noticed you are a bit pale lately. But we can't expect to make a robust Rose out of you all at once. You feel all right, don't you?"

"Oh, yes, thank you. I have a little headache, the reds and pinks glare so, I guess they hurt the eyes a little," Rose qualified.

"They do indeed," agreed Mrs. Cosgrove. "Have you heard from your folks?"

"Yes, I had a letter to-day," answered Rose truthfully. "They are getting along splendidly, and father says he thinks he will soon have a good place for me."

"That's fine. We are glad to have you with us, Rose, but with your own folks will be better, when things get all nicely fixed up."

"Yes," put in Molly. "When you go off to take your own place now, Rose, you will understand American ways much better than you did when you came. And wherever you go, I am going to send word ahead to the Girl Scouts so that you may join at once and keep up your training. Our own troop is going to organize to-morrow night. We are going to call ourselves the Venture Troop, as we will be the first troop yet formed in a manufacturing plant."

"Then the Franklin's will be organized before the True Treds take in the mill girls of Flosston?" queried Rose.

"They also meet this week to initiate a group of a dozen girls from Fluffdown. These are to be scattered in two troops and they will try the plan of putting the strangers in with the girls who have had scout experience. You see, we have no troop at all in Franklin, and I am ambitious to have the first formed of our own girls exclusively. They are very enthusiastic."

"I will be sorry if I have to go away," Rose murmured, and her eyes darkened into violet tones with deeper emotion.

"And I can't tell you how I shall miss you if you do have to go," spoke Molly. "But you are not gone yet. At least you will be made a troop leader before you go from Franklin. Then, in your new surroundings you will be able to assist others to do what you have seen done here."

"I never knew how much girls could help girls until I saw the scouts at that meeting the other night," said Rose, a note of sadness in her subdued voice. "If only I had such a chance before — before — "

"No regrets. Remember all our trials bring compensations. For instance, if you had not made the mistake of leaving home that night, you would never, perhaps, have met the Cosgroves," and she smiled happily in an attempt to cheer the drooping spirits of the girl sitting opposite, who had not touched her cake or even sipped her tea.

"Yet I did not do it. My mistake was not the — the real clue," Rose managed to say, her hold on useful English betraying its uncertain foundation. "It was your mother's good nature, not my mistake," she clarified.

"I'll accept the honors. Drink your tea and take your cake. It is not much of a compliment to turn aside from the cake I gave up the home lecture this afternoon to bake for you two. Marty is gone out of town on business, and won't be back for three days, and our big officer wants pie, and scorns cake. So you see it is the plain duty of you two to eat this," and Mrs. Cosgrove helped herself to a real sample of the iced pyramid.

"I cannot help thinking of that girl who ran off with the crippled children's money," Molly reverted to the earlier conversation. "I don't believe she was a girl scout at all," she declared emphatically.

"But the paper said she was," Rose spoke, fearing her voice would shake her into a full confession of her own conspiracy to shield Tessie.

"Oh, no, it did not state she was a scout," Molly corrected, "the paragraph read she claimed to be. There is a great difference."

"Well, it is very queer our own good officer," meaning Jim Cosgrove, "never found trace of that girl. She must have covered her tracks in some unusual way," declared Mrs. Cosgrove, "for Jim is not one to be easily fooled. So Rose, if you are not going out I am sure you will be glad to help with the tea things. Molly, I pressed your waist when I had the irons for Marty's neckties, so I treated you as well."

"Momsey, you are perfect in your plans. Never use an iron for one without applying it to the other. And I will be joyous in my fresh blouse. Rose, please put a tag on my piece of cake, I'll enjoy that end when I come in. I have only a little time to get ready now, as I must make out a programme for our preliminary drill. I'll tell you all about it, Rose. Take a walk when you finish helping mother. You don't get any too much air, you know," and Molly hummed her newest waltz song as she capered around in preparation for the evening's activities. Molly was always jolly, if not singing she would be "chirping" as her brother Martin termed the queer sort of lispy whistle she indulged in, and even while dressing, it was a practice of hers to vary the operations with home-made jazz.

During all this Rose was making up her mind to go straight out in the big world and find Tessie Wartliz. She did not know just how she would set about it, but her mind was made up on the one important point, namely, that the finding must be undertaken and at once. Rose could no longer stand the misery of secrecy concerning the lost scout pin. Every headline in a paper glared out at her as if threatening to expose her guilty knowledge. Every letter she received through the busy little post-office sent a frightened chill over her delicate form, and now she felt certain her benefactors, the Cosgrove family, must know she had heard from the runaway girl, and they were too generous to ask a single question concerning the matter. They trusted her, and she must deceive them!

71

"I will have to say that mother has sent for me," she decided after a bitter hour alone in her room, "and when I find Tessie— —"

She paused. She was baffled! What would she do if she did find

Tessie?

CHAPTER XII

TESSIE

Again our scene shifts, and, as in the screen play, that retrospective distant picture brings one back to an earlier vision, so from the distance we now see the runaway, Tessie.

Step by step, along the dark, uncertain road of offences which in themselves were trivial, but which brought such dire results upon the erring girl as to make her all but an outcast, Tessie, after the first foolish blunder, found herself confronted with a seeming necessity for keeping up the false role she had almost unwittingly assumed. The girl was not wicked. Her untrained and unrestrained tongue was her worst enemy, and it very often belied her honest, generous heart.

In inducing Dagmar to leave home she actually believed she was assisting a friend — her intention was to better that friend's circumstances, but the methods! How could she know that right could not result from deliberate wrong! That doctrine had never been made a part of such education as she had the opportunity of acquiring. True, the girl learned right from wrong, also her religion was very clear on the point, but she could not then believe it was wrong to fly from the horrors of mill drudgery, made unbearable by the more intimate environment of a miserable home.

So Tessie Wartliz was suffering from an inherited disease commonly called "Greed." Her parents were greedy for money, and she was greedy for good times. She wanted much of anything she enjoyed, and had little care how that abnormal amount was obtained.

The fatal night she and Dagmar (now our own Rose Dixon) landed so suddenly in Franklin, where the jitney dropped them almost into the arms of Officer Cosgrove, Tessie, as we will remember, escaped, and carried with her the pocketbook she had been carrying for her companion, and in that little soiled purse was the much- prized, lost and found, scout badge of merit.

73

Tessie at first thought little or nothing of the trinket. As she had scoffed at its purpose, when Rose respected it, so she brushed it aside as of no importance when she emptied the pitiful pittance of her forsaken companion into her own pocketbook, when forced to use the funds or beg from strangers.

On the step of the last jitney that rumbled through Franklin making no stops, and being entirely unoccupied by passengers, Tessie managed to hide as the car slowed up at a turn, and later she crawled inside, when the sleepy driver, his day and night work finished, allowed the motor to "take its head" as we might say to a horse-drawn vehicle. Her heart almost ceased beating when the officer who commanded the line between the two villages, stopped Frank and demanded to know if he carried any passengers.

"Three empty dinner pails that came out full of supper," the driver called back, and Tessie actually under the seat, felt free to breathe again and keep watch for some turn where a kindly house light might gleam out to save her from a dreaded night, under a tree or behind some rugged, wild world shelter.

Just as Frank, the driver, slowed down, preparatory to turning for the big shed, under which the modern carry-all would be laid up until daylight next morning, Tessie decided she would ask this rustic to assist her. Believing that most men, especially those not too old, were apt to be kind-hearted or maybe "softhearted," she climbed from her hiding place, and timidly tapped Frank on his astonished shoulder.

"Gosh!" he exclaimed, "where'd you come from?"

"I lost my way!" she answered not altogether untruthfully. "Can you help me? Where do you live?"

"Say," Frank challenged, "you look pretty near big enough to talk to traffic cops. How'd you get in this boat, anyhow?"

His voice was not friendly. That anyone should have climbed into the "Ark" without signalling him was evidently opposed to his sense of humor. Tessie did not reply as glibly as she had intended to. Instead she threw herself on his mercy, as actors might say in melodrama.

"Honest I did get lost. I'm on my way to the Woolston mills, and I missed so many trains, and caught so many jitneys I lost count. Then, when I saw you come along I was so glad I almost—well, I just flopped. I was dog-tired. First I hailed you, but you were dozing I guess, then I was scared to death you would jolt by and leave me, so I had to climb on."

"Oh," replied Frank, not altogether convinced, but evidently on the way to conviction. "I did fall off a little, I'm out since four A.M. Now, young lady, what's your idea of fixin' for the night? My old lady, meaning a first-rate little mother, is awful strict about girls ridin' in this bus not accompanied by their parents, and I don't see my way clear to tote you home at this unearthly hour. I see by—the make-up" (with an inclusive glance over the now thoroughly frightened Tessie) "that you are a mill girl, and I know they are takin' on new hands at Woolston's, so that sounds natural, but findin' you like this in the Ark—even mother might think that a little bit stretched."

"Well, tell me the name of some one out this way, and I can say

I'm goin' there, and you can fix it by objectin' to takin' me.

Say, you didn't know when I got on how far I wanted to go."

"Some cute little fixer, you are," Frank admitted, and this was the story Tessie clung to when Frank Apgar brought the girl into his mother's house a few minutes later.

Thus began her adventure weeks ago. Each day and every night adding new and more serious complications to the seemingly innocent quest for a broader life than could be lived in the mill end of Flosston, Tessie was compelled to add falsehood to fabrication, to bear out her original story, and save herself from being "picked up" and forcibly returned to her parents.

She knew the Franklin officer would trace her easily if she went by frequented ways, so instead of looking for work in a mill she sought and obtained employment in a family of rather influential suburbanites. The scarcity of domestic help assisted her in this enterprise, and being really skilled in handling machinery and materials, it was not difficult for her to follow orders, and assist a cook who was overjoyed to have help of any sort in the big country residence.

But the little human butterfly had tried her wings, and she very quickly found life at Appleton too tame for her liking. Directly upon receiving pay for her first two weeks of service, Tessie (her assumed name meant nothing to her or to us) said good-bye to Rebecca the cook, and taking no chances with members of the family who were "interested in her," she left Appleton and journeyed forth again.

She had now acquired a new accomplishment. She could serve as waitress or second girl, and this advantage almost assured her of success in any sort of well-built community.

But it would be tame, slow, as Tessie figured it out, and only a big city could possibly satisfy her ambition "to be somebody."

Then came the temptation which resulted so disastrously.

Out in Elmhurst, her next stop, a troop of girl scouts was drilling when she stepped off the train. New clothes and a better appearance, the result of that first pay at housework, had converted the mill girl into quite an attractive young lady, and as she waited at the pretty little square, watching the girl scouts drill, something like envy possessed her.

Why did they always seem so settled, so prosperous and satisfied! What was there in a mere society that could do all that for any girl?

This question she asked almost audibly, for her lips moved and her face betrayed a puzzled and aggressive look of defiance.

It was always that way with Tessie. She fought first and investigated later. This unfortunate characteristic was responsible for much of her perversity. She set herself against conditions instead of trying to overcome them.

Never had her unhappy self felt more aggressive than now, as she watched those girl scouts drill, every peal of laughter they sent over the velvet green seemed to hiss at her, and every graceful valiant maneuver of wig-wagging or physical drill added deeper envy to her smoldering jealousy.

"That's the kind of thing Dagmar likes," she told herself. "Pity some movie man couldn't get that picture. It would go fine at a Sunday School mixup."

This last was another thrust at organized authority, but the thought of Dagmar recalled the scout badge.

"Humph!" she scoffed. "Guess I could fool them if I wanted to.

I'll bet none of them has this grand marshall headlight!"

Her hand was on the little bag wherein lay that badge. Its pin was entangled in threads of torn handkerchiefs, and its pretty clover leaf was enameled with caked face powder and candy dust.

For a few moments she considered slipping her hand in the bag and quickly pinning the badge on her pretty rose-colored sweater. Then she could walk over to the drilling troop, and introduce herself as a visiting scout, sure to be made welcome in Elmhurst.

"But they might catch me on their sign language," she decided. "Guess I better wait until I get on to some of their deaf and dumb stuff."

So for the moment she was saved, but the temptation was too alluring to be easily vanquished. It was certain to return, and that in an hour when seeming necessity offered a more urgent excuse for its fulfillment. The scout badge in hands unconsecrated was like a holy thing surrounded by evil—it would maintain its own pure character unsullied, but evil mocked it—and the good, like a frightened little fairy, hid itself deep in girl-scout idealism, waiting for rescue.

Tessie was restive and unhappy. She had failed to gain by all her risks and daring adventure. Not only had she lost her place, but she had likewise lost her companions, and while unwilling to admit it the girl felt keenly the separation from Dagmar.

"All the same," she declared, taking a last look at the girls in their brown uniforms on the green square, "I'll be one of them some day. They don't have to be too particular about girls they are supposed to help. I'll give them a good chance to help little old Tessie," and with that prophetic statement, more important to her than the unhappy girl had any way of guessing, Tessie tried for one more "place" to earn a little more money, that she might eventually make her way toward a big city.

CHAPTER XIII

BROKEN FAITH

Following the directions given in her little printed slip cut from the "Help Wanted" column in the Leader, Tessie had no trouble in finding the place offered in such glowing terms. Every sort of inducement was held out in the printed lines, for obtaining help was a problem affording the most original methods of advertising, and each month wages seemed to climb another round in the ladder of higher salaries. The term "wages" went by the boards when the fifty-dollar-a-month notch was knocked in prosperity's payroll.

The position, it was not the old time "situation," demanded little of the applicant in the way of reference, and Tessie, already wise in her new craft-knew well a telephone call from Mrs. Elmwood to Mrs. Appleton would be sufficient guarantee of her honesty. She had been strictly honest even to the point of picking up a few scattered dimes, ostensibly dropped accidently, but really set down as "bait" to test her honesty. She was also very wise for so inexperienced a girl.

So with affirmative smiles the erstwhile employer engaged the nice-looking, bright-looking young girl, whose olive skin and dark eyes made her pretty, if a bit foreign and rather saucy.

"If Dagmar could see me now!" she mocked, patting the lace butterfly cap on her neat hair and smoothing the lace sample of an apron in the most approved screen world style. "This dress must have been made for me, it fits so well," she commented, twirling around in front of the modern mirror furnished in the second maid's room, "and this house suits me very well," with a glance at the fine fixings all about her. "Now for the china and silver. I'll bet I'll surprise this shebang with my knowledge of right and left, and my juggling with the forks and spoons. A new place is all right while it's new, but it gets old awful quick after — well, after pay day."

The black dress was stylishly short and gave Tessie a very chic appearance, in fact although she was seventeen years she looked much younger in the uniform, and she knew it.

Inevitably among the members of that household were two young girls from the scout troop she had seen drilling that afternoon, and quite as inevitably the table talk was entirely of the drill and other scout activities.

It was all so simple after that. There in the sisters' rooms were scout manuals, and these little blue books gave Tessie all the information she needed. Each day while arranging the rooms she was able to learn a lesson, and just when her statement was sure to make the best effect she treated the girls to a story of her "girl scout work." It was just like real fiction to Tessie, while Marcia and Phillis Osborne could hardly believe their pretty puff-hidden ears that they should have right in their own home a real girl scout who had won a merit badge! Tessie positively declined to discuss the "brave deed" she had consummated to obtain that badge, also she refused just as positively to take any part in the scout work of Elmhurst. It was delectable to have the girls beg her to come to drill, and assure her no one need know she was employed as a waitress.

But Tessie "adored the pose" as she learned to think herself, and she had no idea of being caught in the official net of a scout meeting, where all sorts of questions might be asked, the answers to which could not even be hinted at in a scout manual.

Alma Benitz was the name she chose that night when Frank Apgar escorted her from his "ark" to his mother's hospitality, and that means of identification was serving her beautifully in the home of Mrs. J. Bennington Osborne, Terrace End, Elmhurst.

It was all perfectly thrilling and Tessie felt each day she mingled her "better days' smile" with a sob or a grin, for the benefit of her sympathetic spectators, she would have given a week's pay to have Dagmar seen the "hit" she was making.

"They'll be giving me French lessons if I don't watch out," she told her looking-glass one night, and the confidential mirror noticed the new girl actually sounded her "gs." Tessie was an apt pupil, but brains more than hands need training to execute exact science of "putting things over" all the time.

Also a chain is only as strong as its weakest link, and the weakest link in this adventurer's chain was the fact that she had no means of communicating with her own folks or Dagmar, and receiving any reply from them. She knew her own father too well to risk letting him know anything of her whereabouts, and her two letters to Dagmar could not be answered for lack of address. Now Tessie had new clothes, and she would soon have more money — if only she could get hold of Dagmar, and start off again on that trip to the big city.

"Maybe the poor kid's in jail," she reflected. "She's just the kind to get sent up to one of those dumps where they train girls! Train them!" she repeated mockingly. "Swell training a girl gets behind bars!

"But it would cost twenty-five dollars for both of us, and I'll never live through earning that here," she followed. This general summing up of the situation took place in her room, the night before her first "afternoon off" and suppose — just suppose she took a bunch of those scout tickets, and went out to the next town and sold them! She might use that money to send to Dagmar and replace it with her next week's pay!

So there was the temptation.

And she did not realize its dangers.

Nothing had ever been easier. Everyone wanted tickets for the Violet Shut-in Benefit and every ticket brought fifty cents to the attractive girl wearing the scout badge of merit.

"I call this luck, the kind that grows on bushes," she was thinking, as in that strange town she hurried from door to door with the violet bits of pasteboard that were printed to bring cheer to the Shut Ins.

"Of course I'll replace this at once," she also decided. "I wouldn't really touch a cent of this, even for one day, only I must get Daggie out of her trouble wherever she is. It isn't fair to leave her all alone to face the music."

Then came the thought of the possible joy she might experience if she could but surprise Phyllis and Marcia with the sale of all their tickets!

Still another consideration. Each girl was obliged to sell in a certain territory and she was covering enough ground for the whole troop.

"I guess I'm out of luck," she decided, "but this isn't so bad. I believe I'd make a hit as a first rate book agent. Maybe I'll try that next."

It was important that all her ground should be covered before the public school would be dismissed, hence she quickened her steps, and she had but two more tickets to dispose of when the rumbling of a jitney attracted her attention.

It was Frank Apgar on the high front seat of his Ark.

"Without thought of danger, and only the prospect of a pleasant chat with someone she knew, Tessie hailed Frank and climbed to the seat beside him.

"Oh, I'm so glad to see you, Frank! How's the good old lady who saved my life? I'll always remember her as my guardian angel. And boy, those flap-jacks!"

"Mother's fine and she always asks if I see you. Now I'll have a report to make," and he stared so at Tessie she felt uncomfortable.

"What are you looking at?" she asked, her tone of voice condoning the rudeness of her words.

"I'm just thinkin' you look a lot like some one I've been asked to watch for. Did you light in from Flosston the night you crawled on this Ark without botherin' the gong or brakes?"

For a single second Tessie felt her fright would betray her. Then recovering her poise, with the keen necessity so obvious, she laughed a merry laugh empty in ring, but full enough in volume.

"Flosston!" she repeated. "Say, when I get enough money I'm going on an excursion there. I've always had a feeling it must be the original rest cure. But say, Frank, if you want to know more than I can tell you about my history, I have a little book with all the facts in, and even a few baby pictures, I'd like to show you. I have a swell place living out down in Como (opposite direction to the Elmhurst address) and if you tell me what time you're due here tomorrow I'll fetch along my illustrated pedigree!"

"Say, Sis, do you think you're funny, or is it some disease you've got?"

"No, really, Frank, I'm not fooling. I have an album with my name and all that in it, and when I come out for an airing to-morrow I'll just bring it along."

How glad she was she had hidden the scout badge and the two unsold tickets! The velvet bag rather heavy with silver, the proceeds of ticket sales, Tessie handled carefully to avoid jingling.

Here was real danger! If Frank should decide she was the girl from

Flosston—runaway Tessie Wartliz!

"Well, all the same," Frank added, turning on the gas after a slow-down for an old lady with a small boy and a large bundle, "I have some regard for a girl who wants to cut loose and make good. Can't see why a boy always gets away with it, and a girl is slammed behind the shutters if she happens to disagree with the opinions of the town council on the sort of toothbrush best for grown girls! Now, Alma, I promised Jim Cosgrove I'd keep a lookout, and sure thing you do tally with his illustrated funny page he's been handin' out every trip I made since that stowaway ride. I'm durned glad I didn't mention the stowaway. He'd be apt to tear the gears apart to make sure you're not distributed in the lubricating oil. He is sure set on findin' the girl who gave him the slip. Can't stand a little thing like that against his golden record."

Tessie determined to slip off the car at the next side street, and make a detour to hide the route she must take to return to the Osborne home.

"Well, so long, Frank. Here's where I detrain. Maybe I'll see you to-morrow. Give my love to your mother, and I hope you find the runaway girl," and she waved a merry good-bye that seemed to burn the tips of the fingers she shook it from. Tessie was frightened, she was panic stricken! The whole situation was becoming more and more dangerous! She was using an assumed name, she had run away from home, she had deceived the girl scouts, had sold their tickets and—oh, what would she do now if Frank should tell that officer!

Just in time to don her black dress and white cap, Tessie reached the Osborne home. She was so nervous the silver rattled and the china clicked, but the color in her cheeks was ascribed to the "long walk" she had taken "away out Pembroke way."

During dinner Marcia and Phyllis talked continuously about the benefit, and made all their plans for ticket selling. It would be a notable benefit.

Later that evening Mrs. Osborne paid Tessie her first week's wages and complimented her on her "splendid service." She was a woman imbued with the wisdom of a keen appreciation of values, and she knew well the value of encouragement to a young girl like Tessie, but the latter was very miserable, and could scarcely hide the fact.

Now why did the ghost of a small mistake have to haunt her just when everything looked so rosy?

If only her mother and father could be counted on for a reasonable understanding of the whole matter, but the loss of their daughter's wages for so long would surely enrage the avaricious father and anger the unreasonable mother. Not much hope crept into poor Tessie's heart as late that night she packed her little bag, and with many misgivings, overcome only by the strongest resolutions to pay back the money, did she put the ticket proceeds beside her week's wages in the well-worn purse.

The scout badge fairly begged her to reconsider. Its little wreath and clover emblem, the meaning of which Tessie had learned from Marcia's manual, mutely pleaded the cause of honor, and urged her to sacrifice instead of deceit.

But Tessie was frightened and untrained, so that the new reverence, with which she folded that badge in her best ironed handkerchief, was not yet strong enough to call louder than the voice of mockery which hissed of dangers and threatened disgrace.

It was very early next morning that the dew on the hedge was shocked by a passing form making a rude getaway through the hawthorne blossoms, and not even the gardener saw the girl who jumped across the little creek instead of passing over the rustic bridge.

"Something has happened to that girl," insisted Mrs. Osborne. "I am not often mistaken, and I know she is not a common thief. Marcia and Phyllis, you may refund the ticket money privately, and I will consult with father about following up the child." This was the verdict in the Osborne home upon the complex discovery of stolen tickets and missing maid; but in spite of the mother's warning, some one must have trusted some one else with the story, for a brief account was used in the LEADER that night.

So this was the story that surprised the Girl Scouts of Flosston and shocked Rose Dixon.

Surely the strings of our mythical May-pole are winding in a circle of promise and surprise, for Tessie is gone and Rose is going!

Coincidently, out in Flosston our own little girl scouts, Cleo, Grace and Madaline, are worrying their pretty little heads over the mystery of the woodsman who wrote the queer letter.

Would they risk writing and awaiting a reply from the hiding place in the dark little cave of the hollow stone?

CHAPTER XIV

WOODLAND MAGIC

"Oh come on, girls! Don't bother waiting for the big girls. They're going to drill. I can't wait to see the letter, Cleo. Did you get Hal Crane? And will he surely take it for us?"

It was Grace who, dragging Cleo and attempting to lasso Madaline with her book strap, besought her friends to hide away from their companions that they might read the wonderful letter, and then dispatch it to its post box under the stone in the River Bend Woods.

"I'm so excited," Grace confessed. "I honestly do feel, girls, something wonderful will come from our woodman mystery. His letter proves he is nice."

"So you have given up the tramp idea, Grace," Cleo smilingly remarked. "I'm glad of that. I didn't just fancy writing my best stationery letters to some hobo."

"I'm perfectly sure he is a nice clean man," declared Grace, "for there wasn't a smudge on that little note, and I have noticed since that the paper is a fine quality. Oh, I am perfectly sure he is a very nice young man," and the bright-eyed, pink-cheeked girl laughed at her own deductions.

"But Mrs. Johnston's wash?" Madaline reminded her. "What about that?"

"Why, perhaps he didn't steal that at all. He might even have rescued the bag from a real tramp," replied the resourceful Grace.

"Hal is going to meet us at three-thirty down at the stone wall," injected Cleo, "and if you girls want to see this letter before he flies off with it you had best come along. Of course he is coming on his bicycle."

"Oh, yes, let's hear it," pleaded Grace. "I'm sure it's splendid.

I never could have answered that note myself."

Cleo accepted the compliment and the three little second-grade scouts hurried along in the direction of the young willows, behind which an ancient stone wall gave historic prestige to the now modern Flosston.

Nimbly they sprang the wall and quickly they devoured the letter.

It read, from the hands of Grace, as follows:

"DEAR WOODSMAN: We girl scouts of True Tred Troop have decided to answer your letter. Perhaps you need friends. If you do, could we help you? Our rules oblige us to assist all fellow beings in distress. Are you in need of help? You see, we not only can assist others, but in doing so we earn promotion. When one of us tied you up she thought it was brave to do so, but now we feel that may have been a mistake."

Grace paused. She did not like the idea of admitting a mistake even thus remotely.

"Couldn't we leave that out?" she asked Cleo.

"Why, no, how could we apologize and expect to make friends with him if we didn't try to fix that tieing-up business?" Cleo inquired.

"Oh, all right. I like the letter, Cleo. I was only wondering if we couldn't forget that. I'll read the rest. Where was I? Oh, yes, now listen!" and she continued:

"If there is any way we can help you or if you know any girls who would like to join our troop, please leave another letter in this same place.

"Very truly, THREE GIRLS OF TRUE TRED."

There was no time to discuss the last few paragraphs, for Hal

Crane was now seen flying along the macadam road.

"Be sure he knows just where to go," Cleo warned Grace, who had sealed the letter and now stood waiting the courier.

"What's the idea, anyhow?" demanded Hal. "Isn't the post-office good enough for your troop?"

"Oh, you see, Hal," Grace explained, "maybe our friend can't leave the woods."

"Got something the matter that makes him hide out there, and you don't mind exposing me to it?" Hal was laughing good-naturedly. He evidently was just as keen on the adventure as were the girls.

"Now, you have promised to keep our secret, you know, Hal, and we are sure we will find out something awfully interesting if he answers this letter."

"Suppose he gobbles me up?" returned the big boy, thrusting out his right arm expectantly.

"Oh, you know you have scoured and scouted these woods lots of times, and I suppose you know every squirrel by name," Madaline said. "But go on, Hal, and we'll wait here for you till you come back. There may be another letter under the stone," and her cheeks fairly burned in anticipation.

"Well, so long! Take a good look at me, girls. Your cave man may turn me into a monkey or some other forest creature," and waving his free hand, Hal Crane sped off like the modern boy-scout courier he was.

"Nothing could possibly happen to him, do you think?" Grace asked just a little anxiously. The memory of her own thrilling experience in those woods had grown to something like a big black shadow that dragged from her the bag supposed to contain Mrs. Johnston's wash. And Grace also recalled the mysterious note pointed out the fact that the writer still held on to the historic piece of rope Grace had left around the figure at the tree, and, just suppose the man should take revenge on Hal!

"Oh, goosey!" Cleo replied to her expressed fear. "Don't you suppose a boy scout like Hal can take care of himself! Why, when the men went out hunting for little Angelo Botana, Hal was the very bravest of all. He even waded in the swamp knee deep when the men couldn't manage the big drag nets. Why, Hal is as strong as any man," Cleo valiantly insisted.

It was not now a simple matter for the scout girls to occupy their time while awaiting the return of the messenger, even walking the stone wall, and jumping the breaks, usually a popular pastime, seemed flat and uninteresting now to them.

"Let's hunt four-leaf clovers," suggested Madaline, "and we will give any we find to Captain Clark as a new pledge, like our own clover-leaf badge."

"But ours are three-leaf, not four," Cleo reminded her. "Suppose we hunt the oddest, the prettiest, and the biggest number of varieties? See these lovely variegated ones. They come with the pink blossoms. We might mount a whole display of leaves on one of brother's butterfly glasses. I think it would do for a nature study, also."

"Oh, yes, that's a perfectly splendid idea," applauded Grace. "I haven't added a single discovery to my list this whole week."

So absorbed did they become in this newly invented task no one noticed a wheel-chair being driven along the pleasant country footpath. In the chair was a little girl about the age of the scouts — perhaps fourteen years. Her pretty face betrayed not the slightest hint of the infirmity which compelled her to recline in that chair, in fact her cheeks were as pink as the much-lauded color Grace was so often complimented upon, but which to herself seemed rudely healthy.

Directly in line with the three scouts who were crawling through the grass, hunting clovers, the nurse propelling the chair drew her little passenger to the roadside and stopped.

All the girls hunched up on their knees like human "bunnies" and the little girl in the wheel chair laughed outright.

Cleo stared her surprise.

"Oh, please excuse me for laughing," spoke the child, "but you look too cunning — just like — like colored animals," she faltered.

Cleo smiled her forgiveness, while at that moment Madaline shouted the find of the first four-leaf clover.

"And such a lovely big fat one!" she qualified, now skipping over the tall grasses quite kangaroo fashion.

"A four-leaf clover!" exclaimed the girl in the wheel chair as her nurse moved on.

"Oh, why didn't we show it to her!" lamented Cleo. "She can't walk to pick them!"

"But she didn't tell us who she was," objected Grace.

"I don't care. I'm just going to run after her and give her this four-leaf clover," declared the warm-hearted Madaline. "I think we were awfully stiff and snippy," and without waiting for approval she hurried after the disappearing chair, just as it turned into the avenue.

"Would you like this!" offered Madaline, almost breathless as she overtook the two strangers.

"Oh, I should love it!" exclaimed the little girl, the sincerity in her voice and expression vouching for the truth of her simple words.

Madaline wanted to say something else, but feared to touch on the delicate subject of the little girl's infirmity. So she merely smiled, and said she could find plenty more, and that she was a girl scout doing a little nature work.

"Oh, a girl scout!" exclaimed the little invalid, her eyes fairly blazing enthusiasm.

"Yes," replied Madaline, edging away. "We have a lot of fun being scouts. Good-bye!" and she ran off without affording herself a chance to say anything else.

"Did she take it!" asked Grace unnecessarily.

"Yes, and she just loved it. But I couldn't think what to say, and I said we had fun in being scouts, when I saw she couldn't move for any kind of fun. Wasn't that awful?" wailed Madaline.

"No," the practical Cleo assured her embarrassed companion. "It is always well to speak of scout work. Perhaps she will take an interest in it now. But look! Here comes Hal. Oh, I wonder what news he has!"

The girl in the wheel chair was quickly forgotten with the approach of the boy.

"Oh, he has a letter! See how he wags his head!" exclaimed Grace.

"Yep, I got one!" the boy called, now near enough to make himself heard. "Do I hear the good news?" he inquired, handing over the yellow envelope.

"It's for me!" Grace insisted, making sure of the prize.

"It's addressed to the 'Scout Bandit'" announced Hal. "I don't know that I would stand for that, Grace," but the girl, nervously attempting to open the yellow envelope, paid no attention to the insinuation. "Thank you so much, Hal," Cleo had the politeness to express. "Come on over to the bridge, and maybe we will tell you what's in the letter."

"No, thank you," he refused. "I'm due at a baseball practice and late now. So long, girls. Hope you make your points, whatever they are, by all that woodland stuff," and with commendable disregard for possible thrills, Hal turned his wheel in the direction of the ball field.

Now what girl could possibly have resisted the chance of sharing the woodland secret? Yet, being a boy, Hal ignored the offer and happily raced off to his belated ball practice.

"We can all squat down in this patch of grass," suggested Madaline, who, as yet, had not even glimpsed the envelope Grace had passed on to Cleo. "Do let's read it!" she begged impatiently.

91

"All right!" and Grace did squat down beside the others on the little patch of grass that hung over the deep gutter. "Now listen!" (Needless admonition.)

"'Little Bandits,'" she began, "'if you find this I will know you are going to play our game. First I must tell you I have to keep my identity secret for some time yet. My reason for doing so is a worthy one, which I will some day make clear to you. But I am not a lazy tramp, nor a wild woodsman in the ordinary sense, so, if you will keep faith, we can play a wonderful game.'"

Grace paused and breathed audibly.

"There!" she exclaimed. "I knew he would be nice."

"After you decided not to have him a horrid old tramp," teased

Madaline.

"Oh, read it, Grace," Cleo insisted. "What does he want us to do?"

She resumed reading the rather broad sheet that might have been called typewriter paper, if the girls had been familiar with its style.

"Let me see. Oh, yes. 'Will you do something for me?'" she continued reading. "'If you have any little book of your rules and plans, and if you will leave one in the hollow stone for me, some day I will repay you for your confidence.

"'Your victim, "'THE MAN BY THE TREE.'"

"Oh, what can he want a scout book for?" eagerly asked Grace, folding the letter.

"We couldn't give it, without permission—unless, it would be too bad to give away our secret to get permission," pouted Grace.

"We might get permission without telling all about it," suggested Cleo adroitly. "We could say we wanted to influence a stranger, and besides, anyone can buy a manual in the stores."

"Of course," decided Madaline, happy that the secret would not be spoiled. "Perhaps he wants—"

"To be a scout!" roared Grace in one of her gales of laughter.

"Wouldn't it be too funny if he were to fall in love with Captain Clark!"

"And marry her!" topped off Cleo.

"Then your noble deed, Grace, would be noble indeed," added Madaline.

"I guess Miss Clark can marry whom she pleases. She's very pretty."

"And her dad is rich too, so I don't believe we can solve our mystery that way," finished Cleo, and none of the three had quite decided just how she would like to end it when the five o'clock bell from the "Home" out Clinton way chimed a warning hour.

"So late!" exclaimed Grace, "and I have to practice before tea."

"And I have to help mother, for Martha's out," added Madaline.

"Let's run," suggested Cleo, and those who happened to see the trio scampering along never could have guessed they guarded so carefully the mystery of the woodsman's letter.

CHAPTER XV
VENTURE TROOP

The girls of Franklin Mills were finally organized and began work just as Molly Cosgrove had planned. Venture Troop immediately became a band of active, enthusiastic and withal capable girls, bringing to the scout movement a new vigor and promise, the result of individual self-discipline and the indispensible power of personal responsibility.

It must be understood here that girls employed in factories may lack social education, but they are always more self-reliant, more capable of handling emergencies and difficulties, and more surely skilled in precision and mechanical accuracy than are the girls of same age situated in the more fortunate walks of life, the difference in comparison being always in favor of normal conditions, and general education, because of the balance and mental ability acquired through our modern schools and progressive methods.

But the mill girl is never an inferior, and in the exact science of skill, she can easily and at any time outdistance the most brilliant high-school graduate, for skill is her education, and she handles, and fingers, and computes sometimes many thousands of delicate threads, or intricate bits of metal, the slightest fumble of which might throw out of gear a powerful machine. This is applied mathematics, is it not? She uses no pencil nor paper, but counts by allowing one line to overlap another at every five hundred cards, done in some fine print work, and when ten five hundred cards show that almost invisible margin, she knows she has pasted five thousand!

Thus we may realize at the outset that the Venture Troop of Franklin Scouts comprises a formidable array of certain talent, and this must be respected, while education in broader lines is recorded through our little story.

Rose now felt her responsibility with a thrill of delight. Even her anxiety concerning Tessie was allayed in this newly found service. It was no longer a question of one girl, but the matter of many; nor would Rose attempt to desert her post as patrol leader, when the young, eager, enthusiastic members of that troop looked to her for a leadership expected from one who so thoroughly understood their characters.

Lieutenant Cosgrove, now Captain of the Venture Troop, had impressed upon the girl her duties in leading, gently but firmly, along the scout lines, which had been modified to fit in reasonably with the scheme of Americanization.

While it was perfectly true that the parents of Rose would welcome her in the Connecticut town, they had not urged her to leave Franklin, in fact a late letter hinted labor conditions around the Brodix family were not as yet all satisfactorily adjusted, but Dagmar (Rose) "could come if she wanted to," her brother had written. This meant it would be wise for her not to go just yet.

Leaving the meeting room that evening after the organization, and in company with a number of her patrol, Rose quite forgot Tessie, and the stigma of publicity concerning that ticket money, and the possible unlawful use of the lost merit badge.

Buzzing like bees, asking volumes of questions, and pouring out enough suggestions to furnish programmes for troops rather than planning for a single patrol, the girls surrounded Rose with such confidence as to almost sweep the little blonde off her feet. Perhaps her intimacy with Captain Cosgrove placed her in this preferred class, at any rate as a patrol leader Rose found herself both popular and influential.

Mary Furniss insisted on planning a hike for the following Saturday afternoon. Dora Silber believed a long trolley ride would be more enjoyable, while Mona Markovitz urged the formation of a girls' ball team to rival the players of Branchville.

"It's just like having our own union," remarked Jennie Dupre, a pretty little Canadian, "only we are sure to be safe from picket duty in the scouts."

"We're not either," corrected Marie Engelka. "We may have to patrol in case of any local trouble. Wouldn't we look swell in our uniforms?" and she marched on ahead with arm thrust bolt upright in lieu of a gun, while Dora Silber sounded the tattoo of a drum on Mona Markowitz's new straw sailor hat. Mona was short and had to stand the consequences.

"And all the brave things we have to do! Say, Rose, what did you do to get by all those tests?" demanded Erica Jentz.

"Oh, I just studied," faltered Rose, "and then I did without things to send money to the folks. I don't like to talk about sacrifices, but I am only trying to show you what you can do to make good," she finished rather lamely. There was one brave act Rose longed to accomplish, but just then the chances for its undertaking seemed remote.

"Our folks better watch out," cautioned Mary Furniss, "I'm to learn bed-making, and I have to leave home at six-thirty. That means an early dumping for sister Jane, who goes to English School. We always used to call her Jennie, but now she's Jane," and Mary mocked the plain American title with a shrill rising inflection.

"Wasn't it funny how we all laughed on the question of earning fifty cents," remarked Jeanette. "Looked as if we thought earning money was a big joke."

"No, that wasn't it, Jean," corrected Dora. "It was making it fifty cents. Why, that wouldn't tip the 'chink' who irons our shirtwaists," and the original laugh was encored.

"Are your folks all gone from Flosston, Rose?" Mary Furniss inquired, just as the little procession was about to break ranks for respective individual "barracks."

"Oh, yes. Father got good work in Connecticut, and I may go soon," replied Rose frankly.

"You've got a swell boardin' house," commented Nora Noon, the one Irish girl in the new patrol, "and I heard some one say Mrs. Cosgrove was going to start a big lunch-counter for us girls. They call it a cafeteria. Can you picture little Nora sittin' up against anything like that for her corned beef and cabbage!" and the joke epidemic went the usual rounds.

"If anyone could make a lunch counter go, it surely ought to be Mrs. Cosgrove," affirmed Erica Jentz, "for she just keeps her tea- pot going all the time, and my mother says she never lets her cake run out for fear some one would come in between meals."

"Well, it's a sure thing if they come in at meals, they need cake, and if they come in between meals they would be glad to have cake, so it seems to me on that plan Mrs. Cosgrove must need a home bakery," analyzed Dora Silber. "But I'll say, girls, a cafeteria, whatever it is, would be lots better than a lunch-box, and I hope we get it. So long, scouts. Here's where I turn in. Rose, I'll be ready for drill any time you say, if I'm not eatin' or sleepin'. Don't worry about the other 'dooties' of life. S'long, girls! Olive-oil, Jean! That's French for good-bye, isn't it?" and while Jean insisted au revoir was no relation to the term used, the girls paired off, and left Rose with Nora to finish her two more blocks to the Cosgrove cottage.

"I think it will be great for all of us," Nora conceded. "You know, Rose, they're all a jolly lot, but they don't have a great deal of fun. They can laugh at almost anything, but that's because they're so healthy and good natured. I often lend them books. Father has a lot of them, and I do believe our club will be just the thing for all of us," and the girl called Irish, but who was really a solid little American, emphasized her statement by kicking over the only loose stone in the well-tended driveway that bordered the "big house" at Oak Corners.

"Yes, I think it will be fine," agreed Rose. "But I hope I will be able to — to be a wise leader," she qualified.

"That's why Captain Cosgrove selected you," said Nora. "We are to be self-governing, and every member must be a business girl. That's better than being just mill girls," Nora declared. "But it's lots nicer to have a leader who just knows all about us. It will give the girls more courage and all that! Don't you worry about being wise enough. If there is anything to be learned you can count on a double quick education from us, Rosie. Good-night. Tell Mrs. Cosgrove we can smell the doughnuts all ready!" and Nora skipped off in the direction of a gentle light that shone from the reading lamp of Thomas Noon, one time caretaker of a famous Celtic estate, but now plain worker as gateman in Franklin Silk Mills.

Alone for the few moments occupied in reaching the Cosgrove's home, Rose turned the problem of Tessie over and over in her troubled mind. She felt keenly the need of confidence, but could not bring herself to tell this story now to Molly Cosgrove.

"How could I make her understand why I delayed all this time?" she reflected. "No, I must wait for another letter. Perhaps I'll get one to-morrow. Anyhow our new troop is just fine, and I mean to be a real patrol leader," decided the girl, imbued with the same enthusiasm that seemed to permeate the entire girl-scout movement.

Have you ever been called upon to lead others?

Do you know the joy of using your own personal power in a well-organized and carefully directed plan?

If so, you may share the enthusiasm of Rose Dixon, the young patrol leader of Venture Troop of Girl Scouts.

Back once more with her own congenial companions, she almost wished she had not so altered her name. True, Rose Dixon was not far removed from Dagmar Rosika Brodix. Rose was Rosika, and Dixon from the last syllable of Brodix with the usual suffix "on" did not really seem so far from the original, and in the sensational days, when the two towns were stirred up with the gossip of the runaway girls, the change seemed the only plan, but now Rose felt a shadow of deceit in the use of the American name.

"At the same time," she decided finally, "lots of people change to more simple-sounding names, and it was better to start out without that mistake following me. I suppose Tessie has changed her name as often as she does her sleeping places. Poor girl! I do wish she could come back and get a start such as I have."

And another girl in another town was thinking just that in another way.

CHAPTER XVI

MORE MYSTERIES

"I know what we'll do," decided Grace as the three young scouts discussed the secret correspondence with the man o' the woods. "We must tell Margaret Slowden. She knows best and Margy wonders what we are whispering about all the time."

"Yes," promptly agreed Madaline. "I think that is the best plan. Margaret said the other day we were acting as if we had a troop of our own instead of being True Treds."

"We would be perfectly safe in telling Margaret," Cleo followed. "And she can help us best because she has already received a merit badge."

"And lost it," added Grace.

"Received another," amended Madaline.

"I feel a little timid about all the woodsy part," admitted Cleo, "because we haven't any way of finding out about our cave man except spying on him, and that would be so risky it would demerit instead of meriting us. You know we all had to promise to be prudent," she finished.

"But we won't tell the twins," Grace restricted, "that would spoil the whole secret."

So it was arranged that Margaret Slowden should be admitted to the inner circle, and after school that afternoon the marvelous story was told.

Margaret finally gasped. She swallowed something like a tiny bug with the intake. The girls were all squatted in the little tepee made from the school-house shutters, and Margaret always chewed clovers and sweet grass. After a coughing fit she was able to hear the remainder of the weird story of Grace and her man o' the woods.

"And why couldn't you see him?" demanded Margaret.

"Why!" exclaimed the indignant Grace. "Do you think you would be able to take notes on appearances with a coil of rope in one hand and a big slip knot ready to work off in the other, when you had to run around a tree without waking the man!"

"But what did he look like?" demanded the inquisitor.

"All I could see was feet—no, it was shoes—and a hat pulled down."

"All movie men have their hats pulled down," interrupted Margaret.

"Maybe some one was working a camera on the other side of a tree."

"You're just horrid, Margaret," Grace pouted, "and I won't tell you another word about it!"

"Why, Grace, I'm not teasing! You know, all big things like that turn out to be movie stunts—making the pictures, you know. Although, of course, your mystery may be real. But what are you going to do about it?"

"We planned to send the scout book just as, he asked, and then wait, also as he asked, until something happens we don't know what. Then we expect he will reveal his identity," and this last clause had a very dignified tone to the girlish ears.

"That seems perfectly all right," Margaret rendered her verdict, "and none of our rules in any way could oppose that. The only thing is, we girls would be obliged to shun the woods because we are ordered, you know, to avoid unnecessary danger, and cave men are supposed to be very wild and woozy."

Details were all finally arranged, and Hal Crane was to pay one more trip to the woods, there to deposit the small blue book of scout data in the big hollow of the charmed rock.

"Suppose he turns out to be some great man who might give us a new park or something like that," ventured Madaline rather hazily, "then we would all come in for honors, wouldn't we?"

"I would rather come in for the park," Cleo inserted. "We need a few more if we are going to do much drilling this summer."

"That man might be a writer, camping out there, who wants material," speculated Margaret. "You know, the River Bend Wood is considered very romantic. An artist painted the falls once."

"Too snaky for camping, though," objected Cleo. "Well, at any rate, girls, we have got to practice wig-wagging this afternoon, so let's wiggle along. Have you heard all about the Venture Troop, of Franklin? That awfully pretty little blonde girl, who was at our meeting one night, you know, is a patrol leader, and they have wonderful things planned."

"I heard something the other day that gave me the creeps," confessed Margaret. "I wasn't going to say anything about it, but since you all have mysteries, I might as well share mine."

"Oh, what's it about? Scout stuff?" demanded Grace, her cheeks toning up to the excitement key.

"Yes, of course. You all remember the night I lost my precious badge? Well, that was the same night two girls ran away from Flosston. Mother offered all sorts of rewards for the return of my badge, for I did prize it so," and the brown eyes glinted topaz gleams at the memory.

"Oh, yes. We called it your D. S. C. because you got it for guarding the cloakroom the night your brother received his decoration," recalled Cleo.

"Yes, and it was very strange in this town, where every one knew all about it, that I never heard from it since," went on Margaret with a show of considerable importance. "Now here is my mystery. One day last week I received an anonymous letter, just two lines long. It said, 'Don't give up. You will get your badge back some day soon.' Now, why, do you suppose, anyone who has it is holding it?"

"Maybe some of the boys just playing a joke," suggested Grace.

"Oh, no, the boys wouldn't wait all this time for their joke; besides, there's no fun in that," analyzed Margaret. "Please don't say anything about it, girls, but since you told me your secret, I thought I ought to tell you mine. There come the other girls. Come on for the wig-wagging. I just love to stand up on the library steps and wave. Hope Captain Clark gives me that place," and the quartette were off to join forces with others of the True Treds, with their signal flags of red and white.

It was usual to have spectators on wig-wagging practice days, and this afternoon an unusual number seemed to take time to stop and notice the picturesque scouts. The troop girls had worn their uniforms, to school that afternoon, so as to be ready for an early start, and in the glorious sunshine, striking in golden rays through the deep green elms for which the village was noted, the troop girls, with their signal flags, made an attractive picture.

Captain Clark stood far off on a mound of green, waving her "questions," and each girl answered the code as the messages were relayed and transmitted. The younger girls were promptly qualifying, and it was very evident the coming tests for higher degrees would find our especial little friends ready to advance.

Coming down from the terraces where they had been stationed, Grace and Cleo observed a handsome limousine drawn up to the curb where the occupants could have viewed the wig-wagging to advantage.

"Oh, there's that lovely girl that was in the wheel-chair!" exclaimed Madaline.

"I believe she would speak to us if she were near enough," commented Cleo.

"What a stunning car!" added Madaline. "What a pity the little girl cannot walk."

"That's about the way generally," finished Cleo vaguely. "But run! There go Margaret and Winnie McKay," and the bright-eyed, pink- cheeked child, so eagerly watching the girl scouts through the open window of the big gray car, was soon forgotten in the more urgent demands of the wig-wag report.

The lesson had been noted "Satisfactory" and Captain Clark had good reason to be proud of her True Treds.

CHAPTER XVII

JACQUELINE

The words of Frank Apgar still rang in the frightened ears of Tessie, when she stole away from the Osborne place, so very early the following morning. Now her continued failures were assuming discouraging proportions indeed, and she knew the result of "borrowing" that ticket money. She could never hope for a good word of recommendation from Mrs. Osborne, and without it she could not obtain employment. To seek work in the mills now would be equivalent to throwing herself on the mercy of the public, for she knew perfectly well every mill had been notified to watch for her.

To her obsessed mind her faults were now serious beyond belief — she had actually stolen money! What at first seemed a mere matter of "borrowing" until she could work one more little week to pay it back, had suddenly become a crime impossible to atone.

Desperately she tramped through the long country roads, tugging her bag, using it often as a stool to rest on. No one noticed the girl — maids often left employment in Elmhurst and journeyed out to the trolley line just as she was doing.

Childish laughter and the capering of a very white toy poodle dog attracted Tessie's attention, as she stopped in front of the entrance to a very handsome estate. Through the iron rails of a very high fence could be seen the girl responsible for the silvery laughter. She was seated in a small wheel-chair, and at her feet lay a young man lounging on the velvet grass, that was cropped so close the blades looked like a woven tapestry of magic green.

"Now, Jack," Tessie heard the young man say, "I will do all the things thou badest me, but please don't ask a fellow to climb trees. I'm too big for the limbs, and I should hate to break the pretty branches. Necks don't count, of course." His voice was so jolly Tessie listened behind the iron post of the open gateway.

"Well, all right, Prince Charming. I won't ask you to climb the tree, but Jerry—I can hardly wait. Oh, isn't it too wonderful?" and the pretty little girl clapped her hands quite like any ordinary youngster.

Here was Tessie's chance. These were a different sort of people and perhaps they would take her on without any reference!

Acting on the moment's impulse, she picked her bag up and entered the gate. The young man sat bolt upright and seemed inclined to laugh.

"Oh, wherever did you come from?" asked the girl in the chair. "We were just telling fairy stories," and she smiled as if Tessie had been a sequence to the tale.

"I'm looking for work," spoke Tessie bravely, "and this seemed such a big place, do you know if they need any extra help?"

The child shot a volley of meaning glances at the young man. Anyone could have interpreted the code as signifying interest and pleasure.

"We would have to consult the housekeeper," the young man answered quickly. He gave his head a defiant toss, contradicting the joy expressed by his sister.

"Oh, but perhaps—" faltered the girl. "Gerald, don't you think maybe you and I might manage to take this nice girl to work? I'd just love to have a very young person to talk to when I can't have you," and the big blue eyes rolled oceans of appeal into the face of the handsome brother.

"Jack, you know I'm your slave," he answered. "But even I cannot always manage Mrs. Bennet. But we can ask her," smiling at Tessie. "Come along!" He sprang to his position at the wheel-chair. "Mrs. Bennet should be glad enough to grant any favor on so perfect a morning."

"Then don't forget our plans, Jerry," the sister cautioned mysteriously. "If it all works out as I am dreaming, brother, oh, what a glorious time we will have! Come on" — to Tessie — "I'm just going to make Mrs. Bennet take you on. She's awfully particular, but since I haven't been able to walk I just impose on brother Gerald. And he has been so kind," patting the hand resting round her chair, "and couldn't you and I have good times together? What shall I call you?" she asked naively.

"Stacia Wertz," replied Tessie, assuming another name to cover her knowledge of the Osborne situation.

"That's from Anastasia, isn't it?"

"Now, Jacqueline," spoke the brother, "I have to run in town early this morning, so if we are going to storm the Bennet we had best mass for the attack. Suppose we sit here," as they reached a rustic bench, "and prepare our story."

A half-hour later, in spite of all protests from the particular Mrs. Bennet, who as housekeeper for Gerald Douglass and his young sister Jacqueline, had good reason to value her reputation, Tessie (now Stacia) was engaged. Her especial duties were to be with Jacqueline, and Mrs. Bennet deplored to Mr. Gerald the fact that this young girl brought no reference.

"But she is so young, Margaret," he had replied. "I am sure we can supervise. And you know, Jack has been taking a lot of my time lately. Yet the doctor says her ultimate cure depends on her cheerful frame of mind, and she is getting along so beautifully. He expects to try the strength of her limbs in ten days more."

It was this arrangement that won the day for Tessie, and once more the black clouds of anxiety rolled away to disclose a rift of new interest, and a gleam of new-found joy. No one could touch the life of Jacqueline Douglass without sharing its delight. The child, temporarily disabled through an acute ailment, had been enjoying every delight her handsome big brother could procure for her, and even in this almost unbelievable paradise "Jack" remained unspoiled, and her active brain was still capable of inventing new wonders.

The home was nothing short of paradise to Tessie. Even the lovely Osborne home seemed unimportant compared with Glenmoor, the country estate of wealthy Gerald Douglass and his pet sister.

The house was of stone and brick, its trimmings beautifully grained oak and its decorations, all in mellow golds and browns, were as soft yet as varied as the tones of the early chestnut burr. Jacqueline was a russet blonde, just gold enough in her hair to deepen the glints, and with the blue eyes and that incomparable complexion so often associated with "red gold hair," it seemed to Tessie nature had been very partial indeed in bestowing her gifts when Jacqueline Douglass was fashioned.

It was the second day of her service at Glenmore that Tessie overheard her young mistress use the name "Marcia" when calling over the telephone.

"Marcia! Might it be Marcia Osborne!" Tessie almost gasped. Then when she heard further a "good-bye, and Jacqueline hoped they would all have a lovely trip west," Tessie breathed freely. Yes, the Osbornes had planned a trip west, and no doubt they were going. This seemed to Tessie rare good luck. Marcia, Phillis and Mrs. Osborne were surely off for their trip.

"Now I'm going to write Dagmar," decided Tessie—"poor little kid! I feel like a quitter to have left her alone all this time. I wonder if I couldn't go out there and look for her? Everything seems to be blown over, and even mother and father might be glad to see me."

With a girl's unqualified impulse, Tessie quickly wrote an effectionate letter to her mother and sealed in it a five-dollar bill. This would surely prepare the way. Then she wrote a second letter, this one to Dagmar, care of the Flosston post-office, and as the mail for Rose Dixon and Dagmar Brodix was promptly mailed to Mrs. Cosgrove at Franklin, Tessie planned better than she knew in hoping thus to reach her abandoned companion. Her letters finished, Tessie (for the time Stacia) slipped down the palatial hall to the door of Jacqueline's sunset room, to inquire if the young mistress needed any attention. It was one of those prolonged days in early summer when night seems unable to break in on the soft, pelucent shadows of sunset meeting twilight. Tessie found Jacqueline sitting in her Sleepy Hollow chair, the shaded green robes tossed about giving the picture such tones as a pastel might embody.

"Oh, do come in, Stacia," called Jacqueline. "I am just reading this girl scout manual and can't understand these signal tests. Did you ever see one of these manuals?" and again Tessie was confronted with the persistent little blue book which had so conspicuously affected her life.

"I have something you would just love!" exclaimed Tessie, taking impulse from Jacqueline's enthusiasm. "I—that is, a friend of mine found it. It's a merit medal," she had declared almost before she realized what she was about.

"Oh, a real merit badge?" asked Jacqueline. "Not really a genuine badge of merit? Those are all registered and can only be used by the original owners."

"I'll show you," agreed Tessie, and now there was no turning back. The girl, too helpless to share in scout activities, was examining and fondling that merit badge a moment later, and seeing her delight, Tessie felt amply repaid for her generosity.

"I'll tell you!" decided the child, pinning the little wreathed clover leaf on her silk negligee, "I'll keep it carefully, and every day you and I can make our scout pledges. Then, when I know you long enough to be awfully sure you understand it, I am going to let you into a wonderful secret. Won't that be splendid?" and her blue eyes begged confidence from the brown eyes, as both girls thrilled with scout magic.

"Oh, yes, I would love to know your secret," Tessie felt obliged to reply, "and maybe some day we will find the girl who lost the badge."

This ended the transfer of the much-prized emblem, and in giving its story Tessie succeeded in covering the detail of locality by vaguely stating "a girl friend found it and gave it to her." So Jacqueline had no means of knowing of its connection with the Girl Scouts of True Tred Troop.

That night Tessie felt a peculiar relief. It was as if some great burden had been lifted from her. To give to dear Jacqueline anything worthy of her was in itself a thing worth doing, and to make good use of the badge was also an important consideration.

"I never had any luck since I carried that around with me!" she decided, but that was a false statement. There never is, nor never was any question of "luck." The real fact of the matter was simply that Tessie, while in possession of the little badge, was continually reminded of its purpose, and the ideals it stood for, so that in her rather reckless career the emblem confronted her with constant mute appeal.

Meanwhile, Jacqueline refused the urgent demands of her nurse that she retire.

"No, nursie dear. Do be lovely to me tonight," she pleaded, "and let me wait for Jerry. I have the most glorious news for him."

"If all of this nonsense does you good, Jacqueline, I am sure I shall not oppose it," replied the nurse. "But personally, it is beyond my experience. There is Mr. Gerald now. Just ring when you want me."

So Jacqueline was left to tell the handsome big brother about her wonderful acquisition.

The merit badge of True Tred Troop!

CHAPTER XVIII

DAISIES AND DANGERS

In the week following Tessie made a number of acquaintances about Glenmoor, not the least among such being Frank Pierson, the grocer boy, and glad to see a young girl on the big estate, Frank promptly asked Tessie to take a ride out in the country with him some afternoon, and quite as promptly, Tessie accepted the invitation.

"I have to deliver out Flosston way tomorrow," said Frank. "What do you say to coming along?"

"Flosston!" repeated Tessie. She hesitated. Would she risk taking a look at the town in the mill end of which were still located the deserted members of her family?

"What's the matter? Don't you want to go?" pressed Frank, as she withheld her reply.

"Oh, yes, of course I'll go," Tessie answered then, and having said she would go, the question of caution seemed to have solved itself. After all, the grocer would have no business in the factory district, and it would be so good to see the familiar places again. Since her coming to Jacqueline's everything seemed so much brighter, her old fears of capture and perhaps detention in a corrective institution, had almost disappeared, and the prospect of a country ride with Frank Pierson afforded pleasant speculation indeed.

"You may bring me a big bunch of daisies," Jacqueline told her, in granting permission for the afternoon out. "Since you came I have almost lost Jerry. But then, he was so very good, I am sure he should have been given a vacation."

The little grocery wagon did not have to delay for its passenger when next afternoon Prank, with a clean blouse and his cap at exactly the right tilt, called to deliver goods and "collect" Tessie.

Starting out along the broad avenue, Gyp, the brown horse, jauntily drew the light yellow wagon, holding his head up quite as proudly as any flashy cob that passed with the fancy equipage in turn-out for the lovely afternoon driving. Presently, from the fashionable thoroughfare Frank turned into the "Old Road," that wended along railroad and river lines out Flosston way.

"You can drive here," he conceded, handing the reins to Tessie. "I don't have to make another stop for half a mile."

"I used to drive long ago, when I was a little girl with pigtails," she answered, taking the lines. "Gyp is gentle, isn't he?"

"Yep, mostly he is. But he scares up, once in a while. Doesn't like an umbrella shot up under his nose, and I've seen him dance at a postal card flaring up with the wind."

Entering Flosston, Tessie felt more emotion than she expected to experience. That last night in the town, when she and Dagmar waited at the station; their dispute over the road they should take; the finding of the badge, and the return of the girl scouts in search of it: all this surged over her like a cloud, covering the bright sunshine that danced through the trees. Frank evidently observed her preoccupation, for he made frantic efforts to be especially entertaining.

Once, when the post-office clerk emerged from the drug-store, Tessie pulled her hat down until the pin at back tugged viciously in her coil of black hair. That clerk might recognize her, and her folks surely called for mail occasionally. But the clerk never raised his head, as Gyp sauntered along, and it was a relief to make sure that her new and different outfit was a complete disguise. No one would now recognize her as Tessie Wartliz, of Fluffdown Mills.

"I have to get Miss Douglass some daisies. See that lovely field over there! Could we stop long enough for me to gather a bunch?" she asked Frank presently.

"Sure thing!" replied the boy merrily. "I only have to turn in a few more boxes, and then my time's my own. Sometimes I take my sister Bessie when I come out here, and once mother came. But she wanted to knit. Can you beat that: knitting on a grocery wagon?"

"Oh, folks who like it knit in their sleep, I guess," replied Tessie, giving the reins to Frank that he might turn safely into the field over the rough little hill at the roadside.

"And say," went on Frank, "I put a chair in back for ma, and rode along the avenue as innocent as a lamb. Of course I was whistling and can you guess what happened?"

"Mother went out the back way?" asked Tessie.

"Surest thing you know. I looks back, and there went ma and her cane-seat chair, doing a regular cake-walk, along the boulevard. Oh, man! What she didn't say to me!" and Frank shouted a laugh that made Gyp jump clear over the last hillock.

"Best to sit on stationary seats when one goes grocery riding," commented Tessie. "Now I'll pick daisies, and you can whistle all you like."

"But I'm goin' to pick," insisted Frank. "I'll race you," and with the boy's proverbial love of sport, even picking daisies became a novel game.

It took but a short time to fill arms with the plentiful white blossoms, tacked on their green stems with gold buttons, and presently Tessie was ready to embark again, after Frank had deposited both bunches of daisies in an empty box back of the seat.

Out on the road once more, Tessie caught sight of a girl she knew well. It was Nettie Paine, who sold spools of crochet cotton in the little fancy shop, and how glad Tessie would be to stop and buy a few spools just now! She could make such a pretty camisole top—but—no, it would be foolish to take such a risk. So she reluctantly turned her head away from the fancy-goods store.

113

"Now, just one more stop!" Frank announced. "I have to buy some things at the stationers. You hold Gyp in, Stacia. We're quite near the track, and he doesn't love the Limited Express."

But Stacia (or Tessie) allowed the reins to lay loosely in her lap as she watched a girl scout in uniform approach. She was alone and tramped with a sure tread that might have marked her a True Tred had Tessie any knowledge of the troop's name. "Those girls are everywhere," she told herself, and then fell to day dreams of girl scout possibilities.

Buried in thought, Tessie forgot Frank's warning to look out for the express, until a shrill whistle rent the air and Gyp sprang forward, almost tossing the girl from her seat on the wagon.

Frantically she yelled at the little horse to "Whoa!" But on he dashed, and the gates were down directly ahead!

Realizing her danger and leaning forward in her panic of fear, something happened to the rein, for she felt it fall, and even the power of pulling on Gyp's head was now lost.

And the express could be seen rounding the curve!

Prayers rose to Tessie's lips while terror gripped her heart.

Moments were like hours, yet time had no proportion in the fear of death that seemed almost certain.

Then just as the frightened little animal shied clear of a telegraph pole, and with head high in the air seemed to make a final dash, he was suddenly pulled back. The jolt threw Tessie against the side curtain.

The little girl scout—she whom Tessie had noticed but a few minutes before, was now hanging on the reins!

But Gyp was dragging her on. Would she, too, be killed? If some man would only come to their rescue!

Then everything seemed to whirl before Tessie's distorted vision. Things "got black and went out." Next, she felt herself tumble back in the box of daisies.

But Gyp had stopped! The girl scout had pulled him up somehow, and now Frank was there talking, and shouting, and praising the girl who had saved Tessie's life.

"And she wouldn't even give her name," he was calling to Tessie. "Some narrow escape, I'll say. Why, that express no more than shot by when you touched the gates. If you hadn't looked so dead, I might have got that girl's name, but she's in one of those cottages by now. Well, we'll beat it for home," and he turned cautiously into the broader roadway. "Gyp, you'll go on a light diet for this, see if you don't!"

But all the joy of her lovely ride was erased in the perilous experience. And again the influence of the girl scouts forced its way into her uncertain life. Truly the little heroes in that modest uniform deserved such merit badges as the one so lately given to Jacqueline Douglass.

But it would not be wise to recount to the invalid child anything of this wild adventure. This Tessie felt instinctively. Nevertheless, when that night Jacqueline was placed in her dining chair, and while chatting with her brother she proudly displayed the clover leaf pin in a new little velvet case, Tessie wondered what could have been the original feat of heroism for which this badge had been bestowed.

"And the girl who saved my life deserves the highest award," she reflected, "although no one will ever know, I suppose. She risked her own life in the attempt." Such was Tessie's decision, while that little scout was congratulating herself on having really saved a life "without anyone knowing who did it." She had HER secret now and it was delightful to cuddle so securely in her happy little heart.

CHAPTER XIX

THE FLYING SQUADRON

"Oh, Grace, what do you think?" Thus asked Madaline without hint or warning.

"Think? This is no time for thinking," answered Grace, who was busying herself with a complicated system of cords. "I'm trying to puzzle out the best way to demonstrate a sheep-shank knot," and she kept on with her endeavor, flipping the cord ends this way and that, while Madaline, all impatience, looked down at her chum.

"Trying to tie a sheep-shank!" gasped the Bearer of tidings, as she presently proved herself to be. "Why, the very idea! You passed that test long ago — you're no tenderfoot!"

"I know it, but Captain Clark said she was going to ask me to show a new group of candidates some knots, and I thought I'd practice a bit."

"Practice!" repeated Madaline, "well, to use your own words, this is no time to practice. Oh, Grace! I can hardly tell you!"

"Don't tell me it's anything bad!" exclaimed the manipulator of the knots. "Has anything happened? Is Cleo or Margaret —"

"No, no! It isn't anything like that. Cleo and Margaret are all right, and they'll be here in a little while. I ran on ahead to tell you, and Captain Clark is coming, too, with them."

"Well, of all things!" Grace burst out, laying aside the strings. "Something simply must have happened. Do you mean to say the delegation is waiting on me, to inform me that I have been picked out for some signal honor, ahem!" and she rose, bowing elaborately.

"We have all been picked out for signal honor!" bubbled Madaline. "You aren't the only one. Put up that knot business. You can show the tenderfeet when you get back."

"Oh, are we going away?" asked Grace. "Mystery piled on mystery.

Do tell me!"

"I thought I'd get you anxious," laughed Madaline. "Well, it's just this, and it's simply glorious! We're going camping!"

"Camping? Who? When? Where? What, and all the rest of it?" and she fired the questions in a well-aimed volley at her friend.

"Just we four and the Captain, of course," resumed Madaline, seating herself on a mossy log beside Grace, who had selected this seat in the woods as a silent seclusion, there to evolve a scheme for imparting primary knowledge of Girl Scout work, to a group of younger members who had lately joined.

"We called at your house to tell you," continued Madaline, "but your mother said you were over here in the woods, so we came to find you — all four of us. I just ran on ahead — I couldn't wait for the others."

"I'm so glad you did," said Grace, warmly. "But how does it come that we four are picked out from all the troop?"

"Well, I fancy it's because we sort of out-did ourselves in the tests, and helped to get such, a satisfactory report. Captain Clark said she wanted to reward us in some way, and the opportunity came, so she pounced on it, or seized it or grasped it — you know — whatever you properly should do to an opportunity."

"Grasped is the word, I believe," Grace decided. "But what is the opportunity?"

"To go camping," retorted Madaline.

"Friends of Captain Clark have offered her the use of their perfectly gorgeous camp in Allbright Woods. It's a place none of us has ever visited, and well just have scrumptious times. We're to spend the week-end here — just Captain Clark and we four. She asked some of the other girls, but they couldn't make it. Now drop all this knotty business, be joyous, hurry, and get ready. They'll be here in a minute. Isn't that good news?"

"The best ever," assented Grace, and then, as she gathered up her strings, there appeared, coming through the grove of trees, Captain Clark, Margaret and Cleo.

"Whoo-oo!" came the gleeful greeting, and hands fluttered as if conveying, in wig-wag talk, the joyous message.

"Did she tell you, Grace?" cooed Cleo.

"Wasn't that what I sprinted on ahead for?" demanded Madaline.

"And do say you can go!" begged Margaret.

"Is it really so, Captain?" asked Grace, a bit timidly, as if she feared to trust the good news. "Are we going camping?"

"As if a true Girl Scout ever joked!" mocked Madaline.

"Well, I know you of old, before you became a G. S.," retorted Grace.

"Yes, my dear, we are really to spend a week-end in the woods if you can manage it," replied Captain Clark. "Some generous friends of mine, who have been unexpectedly called away from their place for a time, have offered to let me use it. And I could think of no better way of rewarding you four for your faithful work, than to give you this opportunity. I am sorry more could not manage to go, but it could not be arranged. So, Grace, if you will come back with us, and see if your folks will not object, we shall begin our preparations at once."

"Oh, they won't object—not when I talk to them!" declared the girl, in a tone that made the others laugh. "But how do we go; by train!"

"No, we are going in an auto, and all you need to take will be your personal belongings. The camp is stocked with food, and there is even a cook and a caretaker, a colored man and his wife."

"Say, this is camping de luxe!" exclaimed Cleo. "Wouldn't it be more fun to rough it?"

"It will be rough enough," asserted the Captain. "We shall be allowed to cook for ourselves if we choose, but the helpers are there in case of emergency."

"In case the eggs refuse to scramble," murmured Margaret.

"Something like that, yes," assented Captain Clark.

As had been expected and hoped, there was no objection raised at the home of Grace, and two days later found the happy four, under the guidance of Captain Clark, on their way to Camp Nomoko, in the Allbright Woods. It was the best reward that could have been devised for the girls, and they expressed genuine sorrow at the fate of others of True Tred who must be left behind for one reason or another. But the girls of the troop were not to be exactly desolate during the days their more fortunate friends were camping—Flosston in itself offered many happy opportunities.

"Are the Allbright Woods very wild?" asked Grace, as the auto left the main road and began the trip along a less frequented highway, the day following the inception of the plan.

"Wild enough, I fancy you'll find," said the Captain. "My friends think it an ideal outdoor place in many respects. I hope you will like it."

"Don't worry, please, we shall," declared Margaret.

Each girl took along a small suitcase, filled with such belongings as she thought she would need. These, of course, included their complete scout uniforms, while they wore dresses of plain but serviceable material, which would almost serve the purpose of their khaki outfits, in case they were obliged, for any reason, to lay those aside in camp. It was decided two outfits were necessary, and the uniforms packed easiest.

Captain Clark's friends had even sent their car for the girls to make the trip to Nomoko, so there was really little for the quartette to do except pack up and start. As Cleo had remarked it was almost camping de luxe.

The journey, though enjoyable, was almost lost in the real joy of camping anticipation.

"Here we are!" announced the Captain, after a ride of about four hours in the car, during which time no worse mishap occurred than a blowout, and for this the chauffeur was ready with an already inflated "spare," so little time was lost in replacing the tire.

"Does he stay with us—at camp, I mean?" asked Cleo in a whisper, pointing to the driver, as the car swung into a rough wood road.

"No, he is to go back to his own duties as soon as he leaves us at Nomoko," answered Captain Clark in a low voice. "But he will bring us home Tuesday, when my friends return to their tents."

"And will we be left all alone in the camp, without means of getting out of the woods if we want to go?" asked Margaret.

"Well, I believe there is a branch railroad line about ten miles away," said Captain Clark, "and if we have to—"

"We can walk, of course!" interrupted Cleo. "That's a mere sprint.

A ten-mile hike is a trifle."

"Did you say triffle or truffle?" asked Grace.

"Truffles don't grow here, nothing but mushrooms and toadstools," broke in Margaret. "All Girl Scouts ought to know that!" "Thanks for the information," retorted Grace. "Oh, what a perfectly scrumptious place!" she exclaimed as, after some rather severe jolting and swaying from side to side, the auto came to a stop in the depths of a grove of trees, amid which were pitched several tents and a slab-sided shack; from the stovepipe of the shack smoke drifted, and with it emanated the most appetizing odors.

"This is Nomoko," said Captain Clarke, as she nodded a greeting to the colored caretaker and his wife, the latter appearing in the door of the shack, with a red bandanna handkerchief tied around her kinky head. "I have been here before."

"Are you all right?" asked Zeb, the colored man. "No accidents or nothin'?"

"Nothing at all, Zeb, I'm glad to say," was the Captain's answer.

"We are here right side up with care. And will you tell Mrs.

Nelson that for me," she went on to the chauffeur who, with the

help of Zeb, was lifting out the baggage and valises.

"I will; yes'm," was the reply. "I am to bring them back here

Tuesday morning, and get you. I hope you enjoy your stay."

"Thank you, I know we shall," and the Captain's words found echo in the hearts of the girls.

"Let's go fishing! I see a stream that ought to have fish in!" cried Cleo.

"Let's get our uniforms on and go for a hike. I've never been in these woods before!" cried Margaret.

"Let's see if we can find any specimens — fossils or the like," came from Cleo, who had lately developed a collecting fever.

"Let's eat!" declaimed Grace. "I'm starved!"

"I think the last suggestion is best," decided Captain Clark. "We can soon change into our uniforms, and after a meal, which I judge should be called dinner instead of lunch, we may take a walk, or fish, or hike, or fossilize, as you then elect."

"De dinnah am 'mos' ready," announced Alameda, the colored cook.

"Oh, where have I heard them joyous words before?" cried Cleo, pretending to faint into Margaret's arms.

"I golly! Dem suah am lively li'l gals! Dey suah am!" declared

Zeb, as he went off to get a fresh pail of water at the spring.

Soon the jolly little party, having the really well-appointed camp to themselves, sat down to a wild-wood meal. To say they enjoyed it is putting it mildly—far too mildly; they were "transported with joy," Grace insisted.

"I declare! It's a shame to stay here any longer!" announced Cleo finally, although the joy had not been entirely consumed.

"Do you mean you're ashamed of eating so much?" asked Grace.

"No, but it's a pity to waste this glorious day in, just staying around camp. Let's go down to the brook, river or whatever it is."

"And may we fish?" asked Margaret.

"I think so. I'll ask Zeb if there are some rods that may be trusted to amateurs," replied the Captain.

There were, as it developed, and presently equipped with all that was needed for the sport, the little party set off through the woods, following a direction Zeb gave them to locate the best fishing place.

It was no new experience for the quartette, led by the Captain, to hike through the woods, but something really new awaited them this time, as they soon discovered to their sorrow.

Cleo was in the lead and, after plunging through a rather thick growth of underbrush, she suddenly uttered a cry.

"What is it—a snake?" asked Margaret, who followed.

"If it is, don't get excited," warned the Captain, who heard the exclamation. "There are absolutely no poisonous snakes in this vicinity, and any other kind is more frightened of you than you can possibly be of him, girls," she insisted.

"It isn't snakes!" cried Cleo. "I almost wish it were. Oh, aren't they horrible! Run, girls, run back, or you'll be eaten up!" and she beat such a hasty retreat, meanwhile wildly flinging her arms up and around her head, that she collided with Margaret, and nearly toppled her into a sassafras bush.

"Oh, I feel 'em, too!" Margaret cried. "Oh, what pests!"

"What in the world is the matter?" demanded Grace, from the rear.

"If we're ever going to fish let's get to the water."

"I'm never going to fish if I have to fight such things as these!" cried Cleo. "Back! Back to the tents!"

"What is it?" cried Captain Clark. "Are you girls fooling?"

But a moment later, as she felt herself attacked on hands and face, she realized what it was.

"The flying squadron!" she exclaimed. "We must retreat, girls, and get ammunition. I forgot about these."

"The flying squadron? What does she mean?" murmured Cleo, to whom knowledge had not yet come.

CHAPTER XX

CLEO'S EXPERIMENT

Only a moment or two longer were necessary to acquaint Cleo with the cause of the precipitate retreat not only of her three chums, but Captain Clark as well.

"Go on, Cleo! Turn around and hurry back to camp," directed the

Captain. "We must get the citronella bottle."

"I doubt if that will be of any use," said Margaret, beating herself frantically on the face with her hands. "These are terrible — worse than mosquitoes."

"Oh, it's bugs, is it?" asked Cleo. "Ouch! I should say it was! What are they?" she cried, as she felt stinging pains on her hands and face.

"Not bugs, merely black flies," declared Captain Clark. "I did not know there were any in these woods this year, but this must be a sudden and unexpected visitation of them. My friends said nothing about the pests. We simply can't go on if they are to oppose us."

So back they went to camp, the pesky black flies buzzing all around them, biting whenever they got the chance, and that was frequently enough — too much so the girls voted.

"Dat ar citron stuff ain't gwine goin' do much good, ef dey is de real black flies," asserted Zeb, when he heard the story.

"What is good, then?" asked Margaret. "A smudge," promptly answered Cleo. "Don't you know what it says in our hand book? If citronella won't work, try a smudge, and make it of green cedar branches."

"Good memory in a good cause," said Captain Clark, rubbing her smarting areas. "But any sort of smoke will drive them away. A brisk breeze is the best disperser of flying squadrons, though, whether they be of mosquitoes or black flies. That beats even a smudge, and is much more pleasant."

"Yes, I don't care to look like a ham or a flitch of bacon," murmured Grace. "Oh, how they sting!"

"Better put some witch hazel on," advised Zeb. "Dat's whut we uses heah in camp fo' all kinds of bites, 'ceptin' bee stings, and den ammonia's de only t'ing."

"Don't tell me there are bees here, too!" gasped Margaret.

"Oh, dey don't bodder you much," chuckled Zeb, as he brought out what Cleo described, later, as the germs of a drug store.

There were several bottles, one—containing oil of citronella, and another witch hazel. This last was applied to the girls' wounds first, and did relieve, in a measure, the sting of the bites of the black flies. Then a film of citronella was spread over hands and faces, and a bottle of the pungent mixture was carried along as the Girl Scouts took the trail again, since it was voted that a fish of their own taking must be served for supper.

"It would never do to go back from camp and tell the other girls we didn't catch anything," declared Grace, and the others readily agreed.

The black flies had not followed them back to camp, perhaps because the tents were in the open, where the breeze could sweep around them. But, in spite of the citronella, the party was again attacked by the "flying squadron" as they started for the fishing place.

"It's no use! We can't make it. No sense being all bitten up for a few fish!" declared Madaline, as she made use of the bottle of oil Captain Clark handed her. "They seem to like it!"

And, really, the black flies did. Mosquitoes are not quite so fond of this oily extract of an Indian plant, and if the user does not object to the odor, he can keep himself pretty well protected from the mosquitoes by frequent applications of the stuff.

Black flies, however, are not always affected by it, and a smudge is then the only answer to the problem.

"But maybe Zeb can tell us a place to fish where there aren't so many of the pests," said Captain Clark, as they turned back. "It is simply impossible to go on this way."

Zeb and his wife listened to the stories of the Scouts with sympathy, and Zeb declared that while the place he had selected for them was the best fishing spot, another might be tried, which was more in the open, subject to the grateful sweep of breezes, and, in that case, not so likely to be infested with the pests. The clouds of bites they seemed to greet the girls with, had been nothing short of an air raid, or bombardment.

"Well, let's try it," suggested Cleo. "I don't care as long as I catch one fish, and maybe the new place will be fortified."

"I wishes yo' luck!" murmured Zeb.

So they set off this time in another direction, which led them to a clearing, and there, to their delight, they found no black flies. There were a few mosquitoes, but the citronella took care of them, or, rather drove them off, and soon the lines were in the water, with the bobs floating about.

For the True Treds were not yet in the scientific fishing class, and a cork float was voted the best means of telling when one might have a bite. It seemed the girls were scarcely settled when the signal came.

"I've got one!" suddenly cried Cleo, and she did manage to land, flapping on the grass back of her, a good-sized chub.

"Oh, you're perfectly wonderful!" cried Grace. "However did you do it?"

"My hypnotic eye!" laughed Cleo, as she proceeded, not without some difficulty, to unhook her fish, string it through the gills and put it on a string in a quiet pool to keep fresh. "You can all do it, if you just make goo-oy eyes at them," she joked, casting out again.

It would be going too far to say that they all made catches at once, for Madaline and Captain Clark were out of luck, but the others each caught two, and the Captain declared this would suffice for all.

"There is no use catching more of anything than you actually need," she declared, bribing her girls to leave the fascinating sport.

"And may I cook one of my fish just as I please?" asked Cleo, when they were on their homeward way.

"Why, yes, I suppose so, if Alameda does not object," Captain Clark answered. "But what is your way, Cleo, dear? If you intend to fry it in deep olive oil, I'm afraid—"

"Oh, nothing as elaborate as that," was the laughing reply. "It's just an experiment I want to try. And yet it isn't exactly an experiment, either, for I read how to do it in a camping book. It's baked fish in a mud ball."

"A mud ball!" cried Grace. "That doesn't sound very enticing!"

"Well, it isn't exactly mud, but clean clay," Cleo explained. "And before you plaster the clay around the fish, you cover him with green leaves from the sassafras bush, or some spice leaves. It sounds awfully good, and I think it will look quite artistic."

"Much better than it did at first," agreed Margaret, laughing.

"Fancy muddy fish!"

And when camp was reached, much to the amusement, and the unspoken indignation of Alameda, Cleo was allowed to try her experiment. Zeb cleaned the fish for her—that was all she asked. Then Cleo dug a hole in the soft earth and built in it a fire.

"What I'm going to do," Cleo explained, "is to put a lump of butter inside the whole, cleaned fish. Then I wrap him in leaves and outside of that I put a ball of wet clay. Then I put the fish, clay and all down in the fire, cover it with embers and let it bake."

"A sort of fish-ball," commented Madaline.

"Well, you'll see," said Cleo.

She completed her arrangements, though it was rather messy work, especially the clay covering, but finally she finished and the lump of "mud," as Alameda called it, was put to bake in the fire hole, hot ashes and embers being piled on top.

"Dat's de craziest notion whut I eber hearn tell on," grumbled

Alameda to Zeb. "I'se gwine cook do odder fish in mah own style."

"I guess mebby as how yo' better had," he agreed.

Preparations for the evening meal went on, while Captain Clark and her True Treds tidied themselves after the fishing excursion. Cleo was ready first and took a little run down to where her fire smouldered in the pit.

"How do you tell when it's done?" asked Grace, joining her. "You can't stick a straw in through that clay as you stick a splint in a cake."

"No," admitted Cleo, "but I guess it must be ready now. The book says it doesn't take more than an hour before the fish is baked to a turn, whatever that is."

The four girls stood about the fire hole, wondering how Cleo's experiment would succeed. Captain Clark joined them. She was just going to suggest that perhaps the process was completed, when suddenly there was a loud explosion in the hole.

Up in the air flew blazing and half-burned sticks, ashes and portions of a clay ball, mingled with something white, in flakes.

"Look out!" cried Margaret. But there was no need. All the girls ducked for cover.

"What—what was it?" asked Grace, when the shower of ashes and embers was over, without any casualties.

"I rather think that was the completion of Cleo's experiment," said Captain Clark. "The clay ball exploded, girls."

There was no question about that. Steam, generated inside the mass of wet mud Cleo had plastered about the fish had caused the ball to burst, and it scattered into a hundred fragments, blowing the fish to flakes that were scattered about the surrounding trees and bushes.

"Oh, dear!" sighed Cleo. "I just remember now, I should have made a little hole to let the steam out. Oh, my lovely fish!"

"Never mind," consoled Captain Clark. "You have learned something."

"Yes," sighed Cleo.

"An' hit's a mighty good t'ing I saved de rest ob de fish t' cook in mah own way," murmured Alameda, as she served supper a little later.

And then, amid laughter at Cleo's experiment, they all sat down in the dining tent, and as they ate, evening settled down over camp.

To say that their stay at Nomoko was a delight to the girls is putting it very faintly indeed. They hiked and fished and finally Cleo succeeded in baking a specimen in a clay ball and it was voted most excellent, and credited to her scout record as "home cooking in the woods."

The weather remained delightful, so that the week-end dashed by almost as a single day, so replete was the time with woodland joys.

Tuesday morning came, all too soon, and it was with genuine regret that they pulled up stakes to the extent of pecking grips for the home trip.

"Seems to me," almost grumbled Madaline, "a few days in the woods just about make me want a whole month. Think of going back to Flosston after just learning how to hunt, fish, chase flies — "

"And blow up dug-outs!" assisted Captain Clark. "Well, we really have learned a lot and had a good time, besides, you have each proved valiant to the extent of not being afraid of anything in the woods by day or by night, and that was well worth the trip."

"Please don't give us a bad mark on the black fly contest," pleaded Cleo. "Because you know, in the end, we did conquer them."

The Captain nodded a smiling assent.

In a few minutes they were on their way, making speed time back to Flosston, where the jolly week-enders were soon again plunged into home scouting, just about where they had left off.

That they knew nothing of Jacqueline and Margaret's badge did not signify any lull in their interest of the new troop members among the mill girls, and the fact that Tessie, alone and unknown, was struggling with Scout influence for weal, not for woe, did not deter the little girls of True Tred from unconsciously winding their capering steps in her direction. We left Jacqueline rejoicing over her merit badge and Tessie pondering on her increasing perplexities.

CHAPTER XXI

FORGING AHEAD

Venture troop over in Franklin was making such rapid strides in good scouting that Captain Clark, of True Tred, had reason to warn her troop members to look to their laurels. The advantage of having only one afternoon each week, Saturday, free, rather than being able to plan for any afternoon, seemed to have a stimulating effect, resulting in highly concentrated effort.

Realizing the advantage this movement was bringing to their employees, the directors of the Franklin mills had at last listened to the importunities of Molly Cosgrove, their welfare worker, and the establishment of a cafeteria for the girls' lunchtime was now assured.

And Mrs. Cosgrove was going to direct it!

"Now I'll tell you, Molly," insisted this very popular and good-natured lady. "I'll need some one to handle the cash register, and why can't I have Rose for that neat little piece of work? She's not rugged enough for work in a factory, and you know how splendidly she has turned out. When we first took that child in, without any training and nothing but the inheritance of an honorable disposition, I had my own fears. But I tell you, after all, to be born with character is a wonderful start."

"Indeed it is, Mother," and Molly laughed outright at the well-aimed compliment that sprang back and hit the mother "square in the eyes." With her arm thrown around her mother's neck, Molly admitted her own inheritance in that line had been guaranteed. "It's going to be a wonderful thing for the girls," went on their captain. "The Americanization plan of the scouts is admitted the best we have yet tried out. You should see how eagerly they study now, and how well filled the night classes are! And slang has already been checked up as foolish. Really, Madre mia, I almost fear for our own fortunate American-born classes when I see those of foreign extraction making such progress."

"It is splendid, but after all, daughter, we know America best. How are you making out with the plans of bringing the Brodix family back? I will be glad for Rose's sake when they can be all together again."

"Our superintendent, Mr. Potter, has made inquiries about the standing of both father and son, and they have excellent records," replied Molly. "We hope, of course, the mother won't have to go into the factory again."

"And Rose found that little cottage she was so in love with will be all fixed up by next month. I'll tell you, daughter, your dad will have to hustle to beat you and me, I'm thinking," and with pardonable pride the mother, who had often been termed "Chief of Franklin police," went on with the mending of socks and thrifty patching of fresh clean undergarments.

"I am convinced now the child is cured of her worries," added Molly. "For a time I fancied she was unhappy with us, but now, since she expects her folks back, I almost have to hold her in from buying new furniture and fancy fixings. She is so enthused with the idea of having a real home."

"That's her Americanization sprouting," replied the mother, "but you haven't said what you thought of the plan of making her my cashier."

"Just the thing, of course. I thought you understood that. I'll speak to Miss Nellson to-morrow. To-night we have our first tests. I am anxious to learn how my Venture Troop makes out. Rose has been a faithful little leader."

So it was that broad, generous daylight was breaking in on the anxieties Rose had been suffering from, and almost all her real worries were being dispelled—all but the fear that Tessie might be found guilty of taking that ticket money!

Also the memory of the lost badge never ceased to torment the girl who had so unfortunately handed it over to Tessie with her own modest purse on that eventful night when they both turned away from the much-despised millend of Flosston. It was Rose who gave Margaret Slowden the bunch of roses, we remember, on the occasion of the second presentation of the badge of merit, and it was Rose who wrote that anonymous note to Margaret only a few weeks ago.

Returning from a very dull day at her work, with some cheer at the prospect of an evening at Scout Headquarters, Rose was delighted to receive two letters at the post-office. One was from her brother, who wrote in a happy strain, replying to his sister's inquiries concerning the family's return to Pennsylvania. Both he and his father had been offered their old places back in the Flosston mills, as the labor union had adjusted its difficulties, he wrote, but a better offer had been made from the Franklin mills, and this they had decided to accept. So the Brodix family would not only return, but would take up their places under improved conditions.

"And we will have the dear little old house with all the vines and flowers! Won't mother and father love it!" thought Rose. Two of the girls passing at that moment guessed correctly when they remarked: "Good news in that letter. Sure thing!" for Rose was so occupied with her mail she never noticed the friends passing.

The second letter was from Tessie, as we may have surmised, for it was written two evenings earlier, posted on the day in the evening and therefore had that evening arrived in Franklin. With some anxiety Rose tore open the envelope, and was surprised to see how good quality of the paper upon which the letter was written. A faint scent of perfume added to the pleasant effect, and for a moment Rose was almost bewildered at the change in Tessie's form of correspondence. Could she have seen the circumstances under which the note was written, however her puzzle would have been solved, for the maid's room in the home of Jacqueline Douglass was fitted up with correct stationery for its occupant.

Scanning quickly through the brief note, Rose read that Tessie "had a wonderful place" and if only she knew how Dagmar (Rose) was getting along there would be hardly anything left to worry about.

"I have written to mother," the note continued, and Rose marvelled at the choice of English, "and some day very soon I am going straight back to

Flosston. But there is one big thing I have to do first." (She did not hint it was the refunding of that scout money she must attend to.) "Then, dear old chum, I am coming to have the dandiest reunion with you, you have ever dreamed of! As you see, I have learned a lot of new words — so maybe you won't understand me. Better borrow some one's dictionary and be ready for your swell old pal — Tessie."

"Oh, what a lovely surprise!" Rose could not help exclaiming. "Now I can tell Molly," and only the fact that Molly Cosgrove had gone out early to get ready for tests prevented Rose from immediately putting that resolution into effect.

"But I won't tell Mrs. Cosgrove first," she decided. "It seems more upright to confide in my scout captain."

"You look as if some one had left you a lot of money, Rose," Mrs. Cosgrove joked, as the girl fairly danced around, preparing for her evening at headquarters. "Good news from home, I guess."

"Yes, splendid!" exclaimed Rose. "The folks are all coming back and they have promised not to bring any of the old furniture except the brasses. You know, father's brass candlesticks and flagon are as precious to us as family silver plate is to Americans."

"Oh, I know. Molly is always trying to get a samovar. But your folks, not being Russian, do not use that sort of teapot."

"No, ours is much simpler, but of course I think it is prettier. Well, you know how much I thank you, Mrs. Cosgrove. This house has been like — like a boarding-school to me!" Rose exclaimed, her voice heavy with sincerity.

"That's a fine idea!" and Mrs. Cosgrove laughed heartily. "I never thought of this being a girls' seminary, but if I wasn't so busy with my cafeteria I might take up the question," she concluded. It was not yet time to inform Rose she was to be made cashier of the girls' lunchroom, so that good news was for the moment withheld.

But somehow joy permeated the whole atmosphere, and even at the tests Rose's cheeks fairly burned with suppressed excitement.

CHAPTER XXII

THE WHIRLING MAY-POLE

"Oh, isn't it too mean!" deplored Grace, talking to her chums, Cleo and Madaline, after succeeding in diverting the troublesome brother Benny over to his ballfield. "Hal Crane drove out on his wheel to the woods, as he promised, you know, and not a letter, nor a line, nor a scrap was there," and she dropped her dimpled chin down on her soft white dimity collar, until the top of her curly head slanted like a toboggan hill.

"That isn't what worries me most," interposed Madaline. "It is the fact—the solemn fact," and she rolled her round eyes as if expecting a mote to sail out on a tear—"that not one of our troop has done anything big enough to win the B. C."

"How do you know?" queried Cleo mysteriously. "We don't each of us know what every single member of the troop has done, do we?" "Oh, but we would be sure to hear of anything big enough to win the Bronze Cross," Grace assisted Madaline's argument. "And the True Treds are all so brave and such a fine set of girls! Land knows, I tried hard enough with tieing my man to the tree!" and she indulged in one of her unpredicted gales, "and now to think even he has deserted us!"

"He may—have had to go off for supplies or something," suggested

Cleo. "We can hardly expect a cave man to be always so punctual.

But isn't it lovely about our new member?"

"Yes," answered Grace. "Captain Clark told us last evening every single one passed her tests! Daddy says the mill owners are simply delighted with the change in the employees. You see, the men and boys always had organizations to cheer them along, but the girls and women were not treated like human beings." Grace was usually strong for her own rights and she had developed considerable individuality competing with Benny.

"Here's Margaret. I suppose she expected some—wonderful news, too. Really, girls," gloomed Madaline, "I fear our cave man has deserted us."

Margaret came blithely along, her tam-o'shanter being a little late in seasonable style, but so becoming that the detail was forgotten in the entire effect.

"Heard the news?" she inquired indifferently. Her indifference indicated real importance, always.

"What news?" chorused the trio.

"We're going on a picnic!"

"Where?" encored the chorus.

"Out to River Bend," replied Margaret, making herself picturesque on a tree stump. The conference was being held in a shady lane directly back of the home of Cleo Harris.

"River Bend!" a unanimous exclamation from the others.

"Certainly, why not?"

"Because that's our secret place," protested Grace, the first to come out in solo, "Why couldn't some other place have been chosen?"

"Ask Captain Clark," replied Margaret, with tantalizing exactness, "and of course she won't tell you. You don't suppose one little hollow rock, or even one big wood-man comprises all the natural beauty of River Bend? Think of the canoes out there now! And we may even have a ride in them!"

"That's so, of course," agreed Grace. "The Bend is a lovely pine picnic grove. Who's going?"

"All True Treds. We are going to make it Saturday afternoon so as to include the entire troop" (the term mill girl was studiously avoided), "and besides," continued Margaret, glorying in the importance of her post, "we may have the Venture Troop of Franklin with that pretty little leader, Rose Dixon. All the girls rave about her."

"We never knew how pretty those other girls were until we got a close-up view. That's a movie term, of course, but it fits," Cleo analyzed. "We poor mere Americans can never hope to compete with the girls of foreign parents in the way of eyes. Did you ever see such big, deep, dark eyes as Olga Neilson carries around?" and Cleo exercised her own blue-gray orbs in emulation.

"One lovely thing about our picnic," commented Grace, "we will all wear uniform and look so alike. We will have to depend on our eyes for especial distinction, and as Benny would say, 'I see our finish!' At any rate, since we can't get any more mail from the woods, I guess it's a good idea to go out there and explore again. Perhaps we'll discover the secret of the stone man. Don't you remember, our history tells us the first records were made in crude carvings on stone? Maybe he's the original stone-cutter!" and the laugh that answered did credit to the joke.

Meanwhile preparations for the picnic were being made in a number of localities, and the strings of this story's may-pole are again encircling a broad territory!

Keen with anticipation, Rose and her constituents were trying their uniforms on this the night previous to the "June Walk," and if there had been any doubt concerning the popularity of the scout movement, it must have been dispelled when Venture Troop drilled that Friday night.

Molly Cosgrove was proud of her troop. Never had Americanization seemed so definite in its results. The mothers of many of the girls attended the drill, and it was held in the Public School auditorium to accommodate all the numbers. The foreign women in their queer garb formed a most picturesque background for the uniformed troop, and viewing the scene from the gallery, one might have fancied it the picture of some European reconstruction field, with the battalion of uniformed girls led by Captain Molly Cosgrove "on patrol."

Nora Noon made opportunity to whisper in the pink ears of Rose Dixon the fact that "awards and badges" were going to be conferred on "some of the girls" next day, and Rose felt a suspicion of anxiety at the news.

Had she done anything worthy of award? Was there not always that unhappy memory of the merit badge found in Flosston, and so unfortunately lost again? She was relieved now that an attempt, at least, had been made to acquaint Molly Cosgrove with some few of the facts regarding the disappearance of Tessie Wartliz, but Molly hadn't seemed the least bit surprised, rather she laughed the subject off, as if Rose were making a mountain out of a mole hill. So no mention was made of the Merit Badge.

But now with Nora's news the matter assumed a different aspect. Rose had done her best to develop her patrol, and what if the leaders should offer recognition for this? How awful it would be to have to refuse and confess!

"Break ranks!" rang out the clear voice of the captain, and the call aroused Rose to the situation demanding attention.

Everyone buzzed and chattered, the recreation hour to-night fairly threatened a stampede in jollity, and suppressing the insistent apprehension, Rose joined the merrymakers.

Another circle of "our may-pole" now swings out to the home of Jacqueline Douglass. Here preparations are being made for the most mysterious event, and even Tessie cannot guess the sequel. The nurse has warned Tessie to "keep Miss Jack as quiet as she can," but to follow her instructions rather than oppose her. Mr. Gerald has imparted the same orders, and both chauffeurs have been busy all day, carrying mysterious bundles to the big cars, then dashing off towards town with them.

The epochal Saturday morning had now blazed its trail on the June calendar in a perfect day. Jacqueline received her indispensable attention from Mrs. Bennet and the nurse with a show of impatience.

"Be sure, Stacia (Tessie), my small chair is all ready for the car—the collapsible one, I mean. We must leave for our wonder trip directly after lunch," she cautioned Tessie.

Mr. Gerald Douglass was rambling about, keeping step to his own extemporaneous whistle. He tapped at the door of his sister's dressing room and poked his handsome head in.

"All ready, Sis! Remember your catalogue of promises! You wouldn't have poor Jerry courtmartialed by old Doc Blair, would you? And you know, Jack, I am taking an awful lot of responsibility in this!"

"Don't you worry one little bit, brother mine," replied the girl whose soft light hair was receiving its last touch from skilled hands. "I'll be so good you won't know me, and I feel so splendidly well. When did that old doctor say I could stand up?"

"Very soon, but not just to-day. All right, Jack. I'll be on hand. Any orders?" and he imitated the honorable butler in pose and manner, his thumbs just touching the seams of his trousers and his head thrust back as if complying with the savage demands of a high-priced dentist.

"The car at two," ordered Jacqueline, and with a "well butlered bow" Gerald took himself off.

"You are not to wear your black dress—no uniform to-day, Stacia," Jacqueline told Tessie. "Put on the nicest summer dress you own, that one with the pink flowers. You are to be my companion to-day —and I hope you have a lovely time."

"I'm sure I shall," replied Tessie respectfully, but the whole proceedings were becoming so mysterious she wondered if the plan really did involve Fairyland.

"You look as if you wanted to say something. What is it, Stacia?" asked Jacqueline.

"Oh, I couldn't bother you with it now," replied Tessie, but an envelope in her hand spoke more intelligently.

"No bother at all. I have lots of time. What is it, Stacia?"

"I overheard you say, Miss Jacqueline, that you were treasurer of the Violet Shut Ins, and I have some ticket money belonging to their last benefit. Could I give it to you?" asked Tessie.

"Why, of course you could. Isn't that lovely!" taking her envelope from Tessie's trembling hands. "I always knew we would hear from those lost tickets, and now my accounts are all perfectly straight. Won't Cousin Marcia be pleased!"

"Cousin Marcia!" Tessie could not help repeating, as she all but stumbled from the room in her confusion.

To be rid of that nightmare. To have made complete amends for that ticket money!

Now she could face the world! Now she could go back to Flosston and find Dagmar Brodix!

CHAPTER XXIII

RAINBOW'S END

It was a gala day in Flosston. True Tred Troop and Venture Troop Girl Scouts seemed to comprise a veritable army, as the girls in their brown uniforms congregated and scattered, then scattered and congregated, in that way girls have of imitating the "inimitable" bee.

Long before the hour set for assembly on the green, knots and groups gathered there, and when finally Captain Clark and Captain Cosgrove appeared (we prefer to call each her separate captain), both True Treds and Venture troops were ready and eager to start for River Bend Woods.

Grace, Cleo, Madaline and Margaret had managed to "fall in" in one line, so that the march out was unspoiled by difficulties in conversation, which would have followed any other formation.

"If only—if only—" faltered Grace; then she laughed rather sheepishly.

"But we may see him," surmised Cleo.

"Any man or beast in that woods will come out of his lair when we get there!" predicted Margaret.

"Oh, what a lovely showing! Just look back!" exclaimed Madaline, "and how finely the boy scouts drum and fife. Will they eat all our picnic stuff, do you suppose?"

"Surely Hal Crane is entitled to some," replied Grace, "and there's Benny. He helped me before we got Hal. I shall have to share with him, of course."

"We're starting!" cautioned Cleo. "Look out for your feet. Don't let our line get out of step!"

"The boys aren't going all the way out," said Grace presently. "I just heard a girl say they are only going to escort us to the city line."

"Then we won't have to feed them," Madaline remarked, her words being discounted by the joking tone of her voice.

It was an imposing spectacle, and all Flosston seemed to appreciate the occasion, for windows were jammed with faces, doors were blocked with figures, and even low roofs were spotted with waving, shouting energetic youths. Not since a wartime parade had there been so much excitement, and only a word from the superintendent to the engineer of Fluffdown mills prevented the latter from blowing the big whistle.

"It might make it look too much like a labor parade," the superintendant decided.

Crossing the line from the borough into the county, the escort of boy scouts switched off to Oakleigh, where they were to take up their own special activities, the principal feature of the afternoon being a ball game with the Marvels.

From this point it was but a short distance to hike to River Bend Woods, and nearing the noted territory the four scout girls experienced a sort of thrill. Grace felt something must happen to clear the mystery of her cave correspondent, and the other girls sincerely hoped something would happen.

Just before entering the pine grove the two captains, Clark and

Cosgrove, halted their troops and issued instructions.

No girl was to leave the ranks, no girl was to make any advance, and no girl was to disobey the slightest order until the call for break ranks would be sounded.

These orders were given with precision which indicated some very particular program, and served to "thrill" the quartette with new expectations.

"Some one else is having a picnic!" whispered Grace. "I see a lot of bright things through the trees!"

"Hush!" cautioned Margaret, for the patrol leaders were inspecting each line.

"Now, girls!" called Captain Clark. "When I blow the whistle you are to follow your leaders, and rush forward. No one is to push, or crowd, but to advance in a solid line, battle formation. Then when I blow three whistles, halt instantly!"

The ground was quite clear at this entrance to the woods, and at the command a grand rush forward was so cleverly executed it seemed the line scarcely lost step making the dash.

Then the whistle sounded three times and behold!

"Oh! oh! oh!"

The woods rang with the cries!

What a sight! A woodland play or Fairyland let loose!

Quickly as astonished eyes could separate the view into its component parts, Grace realized the stage was set on her hollow rock!

Then Madaline recognized the Queen seated on her throne was none other than the little girl to whom she had given her four-leaf clover!

While the next moment a figure came from behind the big tree, the tree Grace had tied her victim to, and this was surely the very same man! His suit was that exact brownish mixture—and sure enough he was waving the very piece of rope Grace had tied him with.

It was all glorious, beautiful! The fairy queen was seated on the rock—the throne simply lost in flowers. She wore a robe that sparkled with something like spangled crystals, and she held in her hand a golden wand.

Seated at the foot of the rock was a girl dressed simply and representing the Wayfarer.

And now we have guessed these characters are none other than

Jacqueline and Tessie!

"What a perfectly beautiful picture!" On every lip and tongue were such exclamations, when suddenly from the "victim at the tree" a weird sort of whistle music, made on the most artistically shaped instrument, like the pipes of Pan, sounded through the woodland.

"Oh!" was all Grace could articulate, and with its ejaculation had pinched Cleo's arm into a promising "black and blue!"

After the piper had played his tune Captain Clark gave the signal for the troops to be seated, then she stepped forward and stood on a stone by the side of the Queen's throne.

"This is the end of the rainbow!" began the captain, "and I am sure we are satisfied now that all Fairyland is not limited to books. I want to introduce Miss Jacqueline Douglass," indicating the queen, "and her brother, Mr. Gerald Douglass," pointing to "Pan." "Last spring we took a hike to this wood and one of our members tried to do a humane service by making a capture!"

(Grace felt her cheeks would ignite, but Cleo was trying to reassure her.)

"It is not always what we do, but it is always what we try to do," went on Captain Clark, "and Grace Philow tried to capture a tramp. In the attempt she made fast a staunch friend, for Mr. Douglass now stands as our ally, rather than our victim!"

A shrill blast on his pipes signified "Pan's" agreement, and the troops applauded until the echo came back from the other side of the river.

"I heard the bandit say she was after Mrs. Johnston's wash," Pan declared, with Captain Clark's permission, "and she gave me a merry chase after my 'gob bag.' Little sister Jack and I had been spending an afternoon in the woods, and while she went out to the road in her chair I was to lug the bag. You really are an expert little highwayman, Bandit!" he finished, addressing Grace, who stood right at the end of the line.

"And now I shall ask a word from our queen," announced Captain Clark.

Jacqueline smiled and the girls could not help but exclaim how pretty she was.

"You see I have been unable to walk since last winter," spoke the queen, "and when brother Gerald told me about the woodland girls, I begged him to play out the game, and you see he did. He wrote the letters, and hid them in this rock, then the girls sent the scout I wanted, and oh, it has been altogether so wonderful! We will have to have a real rally to tell you all about it, for the doctors say I will be all right again very soon."

Cheers greeted this news and Jacqueline waved her wand in appreciation.

During all this Tessie was not the one least surprised. In fact, she was so astonished she could no longer keep her place on the rock, and she now whispered to Jacqueline she would like to speak to a friend in the troop.

At almost the same time Rose had discovered Tessie, and she, too, stepped aside when the girl left rock, and the next moment the two girls were clasped in each other's arms.

"Dagmar!"

"Tessie!"

Girls looking on knew nothing of the story of this reunion, but it was plain the captains were in the secret, and they did not call the stranger and the patrol leader back to their places. The emotion these girls were experiencing surely deserved consideration, and so they were left almost to themselves, a little distance from the troops.

"And now we have some True Tred awards to make," again announced the captain. "Venture Troop will make theirs later."

"To Cleo Harris goes the first Bronze Cross awarded our troop!"

There was a shout, cheers, then questions!

"Not only did she save a human life by stopping a runaway horse a few feet from a railway crossing, down the tracks of which was dashing an express, but she thought she had entirely succeeded in hiding her identity.

She did not want the world to know of her deed, but we have discovered it!"

Then, completely dumfounded, Cleo was urged forward, and she acted as she felt, like a girl in a dream, when Captain Clark pinned on her blouse the highest award, the Bronze Cross hanging from its bright red ribbon.

She had won the first B. C.!

Scarcely had the confusion subsided when Grace was called up to receive the merit badge for "successfully spreading scout influence and bringing joy into the life of a disabled child."

Jacqueline had insisted mention be made of the "joy" the woods play had brought to her. So the award was made in that way.

Madaline was admiring Cleo's cross when she heard her name called. Captain Clark announced: "A tiny four-leaf clover picked and bestowed in love as a nature gift is not too small to be recognized, and when Madaline Mower hurried after the wheel-chair of this little queen she touched a secret spring. An honor badge' must mark the result," and the much-astonished Madaline also received an award from the queen.

"And who in this troop lost a merit badge?" joyously asked the queen, as soon as her words could be heard through the growing excitement.

"Oh, I did!" almost shouted Margaret Slowden, rushing forward without waiting to be called.

There was the much-prized merit badge! The one originally bestowed upon her on such an auspicious occasion.

When Captain Clark again pinned it on Margaret's breast it seemed like a blessing that had grown greater by reason of its loss. And how delighted the girls were! It was a clear case of "No questions asked."

Over on a little moss-covered tree stump Tessie and Rose alone knew the complete story of that lost badge, and only their eyes attempted to give an expression to the details.

The call to "fall in ranks" was not sounded for a full hour later, for such a picnic as these girls enjoyed had never been heard of in River Bend Woods.

All the wealth and generosity of Gerald Douglass seemed poured out in his sister's woody banquet; and as we have guessed he was by no means a stranger to the attractive Captain Clark. In fact, the way these two worked to "lay out the spread" caused even the experienced Captain Cosgrove to raise an inquisitorial finger.

And now our mythical May-pole has swung around until its pretty ends all entwine the staff like a monument of mirth.

Rose and Tessie were reunited and nothing but the insistance of Jacqueline that Stacia (this name now became permanent, as did the brief title Dagmar had chosen) stay with her, kept the two companions even temporarily separated by the short distance of two intervening villages.

As Stacia was assisting the queen back to earth, and thence to her big limousine late that afternoon, she overheard Jacqueline telling Captain Cosgrove about the completion of her accounts for the Shut In Benefit.

"Cousin Marcia Osborne went to the coast a week ago," Jacqueline said, "and she told me before she went she knew the returns would be made all right in time. So when Stacia handed me the envelope the other day I wrote her immediately that it was all settled by now."

Then Pan blew a reveille on his pipes and the troops left the woods, so we must leave them, to meet again in the next volume of the Scouts, to be called "The Girl Scouts at Bellair: or, Maid Mary's Awakening."

THE END

147